MW01363117

The Secret of Counting Gifts

Heidi Kreider

copyright 2012
Heidi Kreider
all rights reserved

www.heidikreider.com

published through
CreateSpace
an Amazon Company

dedicated to my warrior friends,
those who have battled breast cancer and won
and those who are currently in the fight

also

to the memory of those
who have gone on ahead...
save a place for me,
I'll be there soon!

chapter 1

“Can I get you anything else, Friend?” I ask, offering her the straw to her ice water.

“No,” Liz replies, taking a small sip. She can hardly swallow. Years of battling cancer have taken their toll on my long time friend.

“Time for gifts?” she rasped. “Here, now?”

“For you, I have all the time in the world. And, yes, your gifts are on their way,” I reply, with a small smile. Liz's time, though, is running out.

Twenty-eight years ago, I met Liz for the first time. Eighteen years young and full of life, we thought we could conquer the world as college freshmen. From the first time we, literally, bumped into each other in the hall of the Williams Dormitory, we have been inseparable. Blissfully, we thought we had forever to live life together. We rented our first apartment together, stood up for each other at our weddings and held each other's babies. She held my hand when I buried my father and I stood with her when her husband walked out. It was I who encouraged Liz to pursue her dream of song writing when she lacked purpose, and it was I who found her agent. When my son was deployed, it was Liz who framed his Army portrait and put it on her mantle. I think Luke is as much her son, as he is mine. And, it was Liz who threw the party when Luke returned from Afghanistan. No one throws a party like Liz. The boundaries of our lives blurred long ago.

"You?" she quietly asks me. Even in her death, she still looks out for me... asking me how I am.

We both know where we stand. Twenty-eight years have not been enough. Yet, twenty-eight years will be all we will have. She will soon go and I will be the one left. Weeks ago, she began the process of letting go. We talked about her last days. She insisted that I gather her "living gifts" as she calls us. She wants her family around her for her last breath. I spent the earlier part of today gathering. Her gifts are on their way. Much to my chagrin, she also made me executor of her estate. It will fall on me to be sure that her funeral is what she has requested... "please don't wear black, no hats and for goodness sake, have a party...with balloons!" And, it will be my responsibility to finish the plans for her daughter, Jenny's, wedding. Jenny has already asked me if I would walk her down the aisle in place of her mother. It's funny that I would even object. As she said... "who else could do it?"

I don't answer Liz's question, of how I'm doing, right away. Silence is our companion. I look at her frail body lying in her big queen bed here at the Estate and I memorize the laugh lines around her eyes. Much is spoken in the quiet. I want to savor this moment because I cannot stop time. Seconds, minutes, hours have blended into weeks, days, and years. Together all of those blur into sweet memories and forgotten stresses that make up a life long friendship.

"I'm okay. The list is long today," I answer.

An understanding passes between us. She knows my list, for she has one, too. Together we count the things for which we are grateful. It was her idea to count. As her sickness progresses, Liz's list gets longer. She has become the most grateful person I know. The days when our lists intersect are my favorite days. I feel, as if, for a moment, I am as grateful as she is. Although, we both know this is hardly true.

"Tell me first," she wheezes. I cringe at her labored breathing. I hate being here with her. Yet, my love for Liz is greater than my hate of her disease.

I chuckle. This is a game we play. Liz first came up with the idea of counting our gratitude gifts together. As the IV dripped the chemo poison, yet again last spring, she read a brilliant book aloud to me. The book spoke to both of us. From that day forth, we began keeping a gratitude journal, and sharing our lists of thanksgiving with each other. Of course, she soon learned not to tell me her gratitude list until I gave her mine. Apparently, I cheat. I didn't realize it was cheating to say, "Oh, I'm grateful for the sunshine, too!" when she said it. She never believed me when I told her that I hadn't thought of it before she mentioned it. Not only is Liz much more grateful than I am, she is also more thoughtful.

"Ok," I say. "Today, November 10, my list is this... you."

"What?" she groans. "Cheater!"

"Well, since I've previously been called a cheater, I figured I might as well behave as one and list you again. Besides, if you would stop interrupting me, I will tell you why I'm listing you twice."

"Go on," she whispers, closing her eyes.

I'm touched anew at how much this dreaded disease has changed my friend. Though still witty and feisty, she no longer has the strength for long banter or conversation. My heart constricts. For a moment, I close my eyes as well. What will I do without her?

"Well, Ms. Elizabeth Renee Ashley-Bower," I begin taking a deep breath, "I am deeply and truly grateful for all you've taught me and all you've been to me. Shall I refresh your memory?"

"Again?" came the moan from the bed next to my chair.

"Yes, again! And, again and again and again," I laugh. "I will tell you this for as long as your ears are willing to listen to it."

"They're listening," she attempts a smile. My eyes fill with tears.

Ours is a friendship filled with tradition. We have Christmas traditions, birthday traditions, Easter and Mother's Day traditions. We revel in tradition and have been known to break out singing "Tradition! Tradition!" from Fiddler on the Roof. Which, of course, embarrasses our children immensely. Liz and I have a habit of developing traditions around just about everything. Now our traditions are coming to an end. Our First Friday pizza tradition started in our early college days and ended last month when Liz could no longer chew well. Counting our gifts has become a tradition, just as telling this story has. When Hospice moved in, ten days ago, we started our last tradition. Each and every night, I tell her our story, these details that we still remember. Together we count all the gifts of gratitude that came along the way. And, as is true to our relationship, we rarely agree on what constitutes a gift.

"Love you, Friend," her voice hardly above a whisper. "Find the secret."

"Secret?" I question, holding her hand. "What secret?"

"Secret of counting gifts," she whispers, closing her eyes

again.

~*~

"There you go. You're all finished with your freshman registration. We're so glad you chose to come here. If you step over to that table there, you will get your dormitory assignment and you can move in," the student hired as the university's welcoming committee pointed to a table a few feet away. "Good luck!"

"Can I help you?" an older woman asked, as I approached the table labeled "housing."

"Ah... yeah... um... my name is Kristen Murphy."

"Murphy, Kristen... you are in Williams Dorm, 3rd floor North, room 312," she read off the master list in front of her. "You should find your resident assistant in the lobby of Williams. Her name is Julie. Here is your key. Replacement cost is $7. Good luck this year!"

I carried my key, my student ID, and the registration packet to my parents' car. My brain felt mushy with information overload. I wondered how I would find my classes, remember all the information that I was just given, and not lose my key. A small part of me wanted to turn around and go home. Instead, my Army chaplain father drove us across campus to Williams Dormitory and to Julie.

"Feels like just yesterday that I went off to college," my mother rambled. "Isn't this exciting for you, Kris? I just know you are going to have such a great time here!"

Fortunately, before I was required to give an answer, my dad found a parking place in front of Williams Dormitory, my new home away from home... or so they say. Home is a concept I had never understood. Because of my father's Army career, our little family moved regularly. We never lived in one house long enough to make it a home, or to even really memorize the address. I lived in many houses. I had never been home.

"Welcome! My name is Julie and I am your RA. That's short for Resident Assistant. Are you ready to get moved in?" A small girl, with a name tag identifying her as 'Julie', cheerfully asked, as we walked through the open lobby doors.

"Oh, great!" I muttered to myself. Perky little Julie belonged on the pep squad as a cheerleader not on the dormitory staff as a resident assistant. She wasn't big enough to be anyone's RA.

"Pardon?" Julie asked.

"Please don't mind our daughter, Julie. She's just tired." Although "being tired" was my mom's excuse for everyone's negative behavior, I was thankful for the excuse and took it.

"Yes, I'm ready," I replied, faking a smile.

chapter 2

"One," Liz whispers.

"Whatever," I smile. "Actually, Mom's little white lie to Julie was a gift in disguise, so we'll count it."

"Of course," she coughed.

"No written list tonight, though. I'm getting too old to be able to read and write at the same time. It's that whole early dementia thing again," I say.

"Gift. No dementia," Liz sputters at her own joke.

I feel my heart skip and my lungs deflate. This is so much harder than I ever anticipated it to be. It takes me a deep breath or two before I can go on with our story.

"You are not as funny as you think you are," I quip back.

A deep sense of humor has seen Liz through some really rocky terrain in life, and in these last months she's turned into quite the comedienne. Before I know it, though, Liz's sputtering laughter turns into her coughing up blood and gasping for breath. This is the part I hate the most... this pretending with humor, while her lungs labor for air. However, she will allow nothing but humor. So, I humor her, while her nurse, Emma, gives her another shot of morphine.

"As soon as Her Highness is ready, I will continue," I say, watching as Emma gives me a knowing glance. She props Liz up with another pillow. Liz's thin frame is enveloped by all the pillows surrounding her up in her big queen bed. She absolutely refused a hospital bed.

"Cheater," Liz wheezes. "I'll sleep."

Liz only agreed to "comfort measures" when she made her first appointment with Hospice a month ago. "*I don't want to spend the last of my life drugged,*" she said confidently. I sat with her at that meeting as she blindly made her wishes known. Neither of us had any idea the struggle that dying could be. Thankful, the Hospice office nurse knew. Wisely, the nurse shared some of her experiences with us, and guided Liz, as she chose how she wanted to live out her last days.

"I know," I smile, "and, if you do fall asleep, I will be here when you wake up."

Slowly her hand reaches for mine, as she falls back against her pillows. Her eyes close again. How many more times, I wonder, will she have the strength to reach? How many more times will she sputter a laugh? My heart hurts. Holding Liz's hand gently, I continue our story, counting the gifts by myself.

~*~

"Your room is down North Hall on the third floor. We can take this elevator here since you are tired," Julie replied.

"Thanks. I didn't realize dorms have elevators. Guess I'm tired from staying up so late packing," I stammered.

I felt gawky and gangly trying to balance my load. In the early morning hours, I had loaded all of my worldly possessions into my parents' car. After a three hour drive and two hours working our way through registration, I was not looking forward to trekking all of my stuff up to 3 North, room 312.

"Excuse me, honey!" I heard my mom's voice. I turned to look just before I heard my art box crash. "Are you okay?"

"MOM!" I yelled. Nibs, ink, pens, pencils, erasers, and more scattered around my feet.

"It's not your mom's fault, it's mine. I'm so sorry. Let me

help."

"No. Really. Please... I'll get them," I said.

I didn't even look to see whose hands were touching my things. My writing and art supplies were my life. My high school art teacher had taught me that we all create art. Some people create art in their music. Others create art in their writing. Still others through their camera lens. Me? My art comes in the form of lettering and drawing. Though I had won a few awards in high school, I drew and lettered for myself. It was my way of relaxing and creating... my way of escaping stress. My supply box held the keys to art for me. It held all the tools I needed. Painstakingly, I had arranged all of the inks and paints, pastels and pencils in the box. In horror, I tried to gather all of my tools before any of it was mistakenly stepped on.

"I understand. Sometimes you just don't want anyone touching your stuff."

I looked up to see her standing there holding my pens. As she handed them back, I knew that I had just met a kindred spirit.

"Thanks for understanding. I'm Kris," I said, holding out my empty hand.

"Liz." she replied, handing back the pens. "And, you're welcome. Where's your room?"

"312," I said.

"Hey, that's just down the hall. I'll help carry your stuff." She smiled, as she picked up a bag.

By the time we reached the door to my room, Liz had managed to endear herself not only to my mother, but also, to my dad. Not an easy task. My life has been spent moving from one base to another, as Dad pursued his army career. Though I deeply loved my father and his Army ways, any friend I had ever had was immediately intimidated by Army Chaplain Donald Murphy.

"My official ranking is Army Chaplain, not Colonel." I heard Dad laugh, as he tried to explain his title to Liz. "Please just call me 'Murph.' All my friends do."

"Ok, Colonel Murph," Liz laughed. Dad rolled his eyes and smiled. Another gift.

"Oh, my," my mom whispered as I unlocked my door. Without looking, I pushed past her to set my bags inside the door and was instantly overwhelmed... with cats.

"Wow," giggled Liz. "This could be interesting."

There have only been a few times, in my life, when I have been at a complete loss for words. I looked around. There were no words to express the horror I felt. The university administration had paired me with a roommate who apparently had quite a love affair with felines. Cat posters, cat figurines, cat curtains, cat this, and cat that... everywhere!

"Ugh. Cats," I moaned. "I really hate cats... real or imagined."

"Now, Kristen," Mom chirped, "you're going to have to learn to get along with everyone."

I bit off a sarcastic reply. In that moment, I realized that the cat room was the lesser of the two evils I faced. I could either live with an unknown feline lover or take my stuff back to the car. I had no desire to go back home and be parented any more. Somehow, in my 18-year-old genius, I thought I was all grown up.

"I know. I know!" I huffed.

"My roommate cancelled," Liz casually mentioned. "We could check with Julie about switching your room." That was the best gift of the day, probably the second best gift of my entire life.

After the initial roommate fiasco was solved, college life was great. Liz and I settled into a comfortable routine. She declared music as her major. She loved every single music theory class she attended. She played guitar, piano, and flute. When she decided she wanted to learn a stringed instrument, she didn't just settle for learning to play the violin. Instead, she mastered the harp. Nothing in life gave Liz more pleasure than making music.

I was tone deaf and had no rhythm. Liz could hardly draw a straight line. We were a perfect match. There was no competition between us. While she pursued her music with a vengeance, I pursued a social work degree. The 18-year-old me was ready to change the world, one child at a time. While I attended classes, seminars, and wrote countless papers, Liz's music became her life. Often she would be the last student in the music room, practicing late into the night. She dated other music majors and went to every recital on campus. My art remained my solace, my respite from the world. While Liz would be out, I would be in.

"You're hiding your light under a bushel," she would say. When I asked her what that meant, she laughed loudly, and said, "I don't know. It's just something my grandma used to say to me."

Throughout our college years, I often felt as if Liz lived life for both of us. Liz was fun and exciting. Everyone loved being with her. Though she adamantly denied it, she was also jaw-droppingly beautiful. She stood at a stately 5 feet 9 inches with a gorgeous athletic build, long dark hair, and brown eyes that danced with joy. She genuinely loved people and loved being with them. She dated often, hardly ever the same guy twice. When I asked her about that, she responded, "I haven't found what I'm looking for."

Neither had I. But, then again, I wasn't trying very hard. Though just an inch shorter than Liz, I found myself hiding in her shadow. I was probably more athletic than Liz, but I would never be described as being gorgeous. I spent my high school years as a swimmer. Thus, I had a swimmer's build. My hair was a plain shade of brown and matched my eyes. Since I was always awkward in a group of people, I was the proverbial wallflower. Plain wallflower, with over-developed arms and shoulders, described me well. In my mind, I was the antithesis to Liz's beauty.

At the end of our freshman year, Liz announced that she was not going home for the summer. The hunt for an apartment began. We called every advertisement we could find. We asked graduating seniors for leads on vacant apartments and we scoured neighborhoods. In the end, the place we found was perfect. A tiny two bedroom attic apartment with dormers and rounded doorways. It had a small galley kitchen and an even smaller bathroom. Standing in the empty living room, for the first time in my life, I felt at home. We paid the deposit. A week later, we both moved in. I called my parents to let them know I was staying with Liz. I signed up for a local summer internship and Liz signed up for summer classes. The apartment wasn't big or fancy. We didn't care. It was home. Another gift.

chapter 3

"Remember air conditioner?" she whispers.

"How could I forget? I still have the scar," I chuckle. "You were so quiet. I thought you were sleeping."

"Nah," came her quiet reply.

"Do you need a drink?" I ask. My concern for Liz runs deep. I don't know how to feel anything but concern. Concern, and a deep sense of pending doom.

"No, cold."

Tucking her hand back under the electric blanket that lay on top of her, I turn up her thermostat a few more degrees. Liz has become so frail that extra blankets cause extra pain. We all adjust the thermostat whenever she asks.

"Thanks," she slurs. She so hates that the pain medicine makes her feel and sound drugged. I am, however, grateful for any relief from the pain that she can get. I silently add “drugs for Liz” to my mental gratitude list.

“I'm heading home, now,” Liz's nurse, Emma, pokes her head into the room. “Liz, do you need anything before I go?”

A small shake of the head is Liz's only reply.

“Ok. Rest well,” Emma answers. “Jana is your nurse on duty now if you do need anything.” I add “Liz's nurses” to the list in my head. Their concern has been a blessing to me as I watch them care for Liz.

“Shall I continue or do you want to sleep?”

“Keep going. Sleep later,” comes her sleepy reply.

“Ok. And, I will add the air conditioner that you dropped on my hand to the list.”

“Bah,” is the only reply from the bed.

~*~

Though we loved that attic apartment, it was as hot as the Sahara in the summer. The first summer, we suffered through the heat with four fans and hourly showers. We vowed that we would save every penny we could find to purchase a window unit for the next summer. And, save we did.

All throughout the fall, winter, and spring, we would drop our change into the big pickle jar that Liz brought home from her job at the diner around the corner. I marveled at Liz's diner job. Liz came from Western New York and old New England money. While I worked three part-time jobs and carried a full class load, Liz worked at the diner and took a partial class load. She didn't have to work. She wanted to work.

"My grandma taught me to work hard and to enjoy every minute of it," she replied, any time I would bring it up.

"I don't hate my job... just my uniform," she would laugh and then strike a pose in her gaudy double-breasted gold dress.

For three years, she endured that ghastly uniform. As well as the old men who drank coffee and gawked at her backside. She said she thought they were just lonely. I thought they were gross. Fortunately for me, the job also included lots of tips which helped fill the pickle jar.

At the beginning of May, the jar could hold no more. On May 5, we spent an evening counting and wrapping pennies, nickels, dimes, and quarters.

"Hey, here's a half dollar. What do you think we should do with this?" Liz asked me, while counting out fifty pennies.

"How many half dollars are in here?" I questioned.

Liz shrugged her shoulders and continued counting. She set the half dollar off to the side. As we sorted, counted, and wrapped the other coins, the little pile of half dollars slowly grew. Seventy minutes later we had $362 wrapped in various coin denominations *and twenty-seven half dollars.*

"I'm starved," Liz exclaimed, kneading the stiff muscles in her neck. "What do we have to eat around here?"

"I think there is still some day-old bread from the diner and a box of mac-n-cheese," I muttered.

"Pizza. I need pizza." Liz sat straight up. "Let's use the half-dollars for pizza!" She picked up the phone and called Village Pizza for delivery. Our First Friday pizza tradition was born.

"Is $362 enough for a window air conditioner?" I asked, while we waited for the pizza delivery.

"I hope so!" she exclaimed. "It ought to be for a tiny little ice box in the window. Do we even know what size unit we need?"

"SMALL!" We blurted together. Everything in our apartment was small. A small unit would be all we needed.

"Monday, I will take all of this," Liz motioned to the pile of wrapped coins, "to the bank. Can you go a/c shopping on Monday?"

"I have class until 4 p.m. and then I work at the Psych Department office until 7. I will probably be back here around 7:20. Want to go then?"

"Sure. I'll see if Dan will take us."

Liz had dated Dan a few times the year before, but their very platonic relationship had settled into a great friendship. I teased Liz when she first brought Dan to the apartment. Liz tended to date very attractive men. Tall and gangly, with red hair and blue eyes, Dan McClintock wasn't one of the more attractive men that Liz had dated. He was a great guy though. I soon came to learn that it was Dan's heart that attracted Liz. He was the nicest guy she had ever met.

They developed a deep and abiding friendship. Perhaps, it was because they were both over-achievers. Maybe they became friends because they shared a "Type-A" personality. Personally, I think the glue that held Dan and Liz together was their need for affirmation. Dan grew up with an alcoholic father who kicked him out of the house on the night of his high school graduation. Liz was raised by a society mother who dressed her up, showed her off, and always expected Liz to be on her best behavior. Neither knew unconditional love. They found that love in each other.

Dan was who we called whenever we needed help. As a poor college student, he worked cheap. All he required was food. As long as we fed him, he was always more than willing to lend a hand.

"Bring home day-old lemon meringue pie and he'll be here," I promised.

Sure enough, Monday evening I walked into the apartment to see Dan sitting at our tag-sale table enjoying half of a day-old pie.

"Diz iz gud," he mumbled around a mouth full of meringue.

"It always is, Dan," I replied. "Thanks for helping!"

"Sure. Where are we going?" he asked before he shoveled in another bite.

"Ask Liz. She's put in the most money. She gets to decide."

"The Warehouse," piped Liz.

Getting to know Liz was an ongoing study in contradictions. Though she had a sports car her parents had given her for her high school graduation gift, she left it at home. Liz never flaunted money or status. She rode the city bus, shopped at resale shops, waited tables, and lived a life pretending that she didn't have a trust fund that was paying for her education. Her life was one I couldn't comprehend.

The three of us piled into Dan's little old truck. He fondly called it "Mighty Truck." Honestly, there wasn't much "mighty" about it. However, it eventually got us where we needed to be. Though I wasn't nearly as fond of Mighty Truck as Dan was, I found myself grateful that we weren't trying to haul an air conditioner onto the bus. When Liz and I began looking back and counting gifts, Mighty Truck made the gratitude list.

"Kris is doing the negotiating tonight, Dan," informed Liz.

"Of course she is," he replied.

I loved negotiating, especially when the bargaining was centered around how much money I would spend on something. My grandfather negotiated everything, from lawn care to new vehicles. I often watched him, eventually learning to haggle almost as well as he did. He would have been proud of me tonight. In the end, we walked out with a new air conditioner unit, and we had enough money left for dinner out and gas for Mighty Truck. If only it had been so easy to get the unit up to the apartment.

We stopped for dinner out. Dan chose the place. Buffet types of eateries were his favorite. Though tall and thin, he definitely got his money's worth any time he went to an all-you-can-eat buffet. I later learned that Dan's homeless summer between high school and college left him hungry on more than one occasion. He worked that summer for a local landscaping company. He slept and showered at a friend's house and biked to work each day. As soon as he got his first paycheck, he bought Mighty Truck. Dan lived in that truck for the remainder of the summer, eating peanut butter and day-old bread. He often ran out of food before his next pay day. I have wondered if all-you-can eat buffets were like a gold mine to him.

By the time we returned to the apartment, with our full bellies, we were all tired. However, since we fed him a huge meal, we still had Dan's help. Liz and I learned, a long time ago, to take advantage of every minute of help that we could get. The three of us staggered and stumbled up the outside steel stairs with the air conditioner.

"Don't drop it!" Liz cautioned. "Be careful, don't bump it! Watch out for that corner! Tip it slightly to the left."

"LIZ!" I yelled.

"What? I'm just trying not to damage our brand spankin' new air conditioner!" she huffed.

"LIZ! My hand is there!"

By tipping the air conditioner to the left, Liz managed to pin my hand against the steel handrail of the staircase and the sharp edge of the air conditioner. I could feel the blood oozing.

"Where?" she glanced around.

"Is your hand where the blood is?" Dan joked.

"YES! And, I'm not laughing! LIZ! Please tip it back to the right... right now!"

"Oh...oh... oh!" was her only reply. Liz has many, many great qualities. Helping in an emergency or seeing blood, though, are not included in her list of admirable traits. After she tipped the unit back to the right, she looked pale and shaky.

"Liz, just go unlock the door," I muttered through clenched teeth.

"Just don't drip blood on the floor," she stammered.

Dan and I managed to get the air conditioner to the living room. Only about fifteen splotches of blood landed on the floor before I found a towel to wrap around my hand. Without a word, all three of us piled back into Mighty Truck. Dan drove me to the campus' 24 hour clinic for seven stitches across my hand.

"Oh, I'm so sorry!" Liz flittered. "Are you okay? Are you

sure? Do you need anything? Can I do anything?"

"LIZ! GET IN!" I bellowed. Apparently, I'm not very nice when I'm in pain. Dan just laughed at both of us and drove us home.

"You owe me another pie," he yelled, as we tumbled out of his truck.

"Tomorrow, Dan," Liz retorted. "Tomorrow."

chapter 4

"I don't flit," she rasps.

"My story, my words," I say, holding her straw again for another weak sip. "You can tell it next time."

"Nah," came the delayed response. We both know that she is far beyond story-telling. We just do not know how far beyond.

"Do you mind if I listen?" Jana, the night nurse, sweetly asks. I am grateful for the change of topic and add it to my ongoing gratitude list.

"We'd love the company," I quietly answer.

"Jenny called ten minutes ago. She's on her way home," Jana informs us. "I'll bring in another chair."

Jenny and I have been taking turns sitting with Liz. Mostly, though, we end up together, sitting in Liz's bedroom... watching and waiting. My husband, Dan, joins us between his hours at the clinic and Luke stops in whenever he can, which is becoming more and more frequent. Tonight, he and Dan are driving to the airport to pick up Liz's son, Mark, who is flying home from the West Coast. Soon we will all be together, and Liz will have all the company she could ever want.

"Did she mention if Mike would be joining her?" I quietly ask Jana.

"She didn't say. Should I plan on him?" she asks back.

"Yes, if you don't mind," I answer.

"Not a problem. I will start another pot of coffee and put the tea kettle on for Jenny," Jana states, walking out of the room.

"Looks like a party is on it's way, Friend," I say, smoothing her blanket. "Are you warm enough?"

A slow nod in the affirmative is her only response.

"Hi Mom," Jenny's tentative voice fills the room. "How's she doing?" she asks me.

"You can ask her yourself. She's awake."

Jenny steps quietly to the other side of Liz's bed. She sits down gently and kisses her mother on the cheek. Liz replies with her signature wink.

"Love you, Mama," Jenny smiles.

"Love you more," Liz whispers.

"Your mom and I are reminiscing and counting gifts again tonight. Care to join us?" I ask Jenny. "Mark, Luke and Dan are on their way back from the airport. They'll be here soon. Is Mike coming?"

"He's on duty until 11 p.m. He said he'd come after his shift," she answers.

Jenny's fiance, Micah Caldwell (Mike to all of us) is a local firefighter and paramedic. When he isn't working his shifts at the firehouse, he works in my husband's clinic as a medical technician. I guess that's the fancy title to say that Mike takes the histories and vital signs for Dr. Daniel McClintock's patients. A few years ago, Dan gave up his partnership at Crawford Family Medicine to pursue his dream of medical missions. He joined an indigent clinic for the uninsured here in Western New York and twice a year the clinic closes for ten days. Dan takes his staff to the mountains of Guatemala to practice medicine there. The very first year, Liz went along. She said it changed her forever. Since that time, she has anonymously funded every single trip. Over the years, she's learned to be grateful for the trust fund that she grew up hating.

"What about Ryan?" Jenny asks, glancing at me. My other son, Ryan, is in his sophomore year at the university on a football scholarship. He and I have talked much over the past few days. Rarely is dying convenient and rarely does death wait for an appropriate moment.

"He'll come when we call. He cut classes and drove over yesterday to give your mom a hug and a kiss." A look of understanding passes between us. Ryan already had his time to say goodbye to his Aunt Liz.

"Please continue the story. I'd love to listen. You know, this is my favorite fairy tale of all time. I don't even know how many times mom has told it to me. However, it's always best when you tell it together," Jenny smiles, reaching for her mother's frail hand. "Has she met my dad yet?"

In the pale evening light, I see the pain reflected in her eyes. Jenny's unfaithful father, Robert, left. He's never come back. The little girl in Jenny's heart still mourns the loss of a father she hardly knew. That same little girl's heart still hopes for the return of Prince Charming.

"I was just getting to that part."

~*~

After the stitches were removed from my hand, Liz and I heaved the air conditioner unit into the only window in the entire apartment that could hold it. Unfortunately, that window was the one window at the end of the galley kitchen. All summer the kitchen felt like a refrigerator and the tiny bathroom on the other end felt like a sauna. However, if we sat, slept, and studied in the living room, we were perfectly content. We haven't forgotten the air conditioner over the years because it helped keep Liz cool the summer she fell in love.

On a steamy July afternoon, Liz waltzed in from her shift at the diner, humming "Someday My Prince Will Come."

"I'm in love," she proudly announced.

"Again?" I jeered.

"You dare mock me?" she quipped. "Those others, they were just practice for falling in love. Mere boys, mind you. Today, I met my man." With that, she sashayed to her room to change out of the atrocious uniform.

"So, what's so great about this MAN?" I hollered at her closed door.

"Everything," was the only reply as she darted into the bathroom. "He's picking me up in ten minutes to go to the senior recital that is on tonight at the Performing Arts Center."

"Wow. A date already, huh? And a free one at that," I huffed jealously. "Wouldn't a real man take you out for Broadway, or dinner, or something nice?" There was no answer from the closed bathroom door. She had already learned to ignore me when I became petty. The only sound I heard was the shower.

Eight and a half minutes later, she emerged no longer looking or smelling like the diner. I attempted to make small talk until the man... pardon me, HER man, arrived.

"So, where did you meet this man?"

"My man?" she asked innocently.

"So sorry," I mocked.

"If you must know, he came into the diner today."

"Serious?" I laughed uproariously. "You seriously fell in love with a diner drop-in?"

"Yes... he stayed all through the lunch rush. After I refilled his coffee for the fourth time, he asked me for a date."

"Liz?" I couldn't believe I was having this conversation with her. "Do you know anything about this guy? Like, for instance, is he related to Charles Manson?"

"You worry much too much!" she giggled. "He's a perfectly nice gentleman. His name is Robert and he's new to the business faculty. Besides, if he's good enough to be hired by the University, he's good enough for me."

"Is he old?" I questioned.

"Not too," she replied to the knock on the door.

Liz rushed to open the door. In walked the man who would eventually crush my friend's spirit. I should have kicked him out right then and there, and locked her back into the bathroom. Isn't it funny how hindsight is always 20/20? However, on that evening of July 7, Robert charmed the socks off of both of us.

"You must be Kris," he said smoothly, holding out his hand.

I shot Liz a look that said, "seriously? He knows my name?!" She only shrugged in return.

"Yes, I am Kris," I flustered. "Obviously, you are Robert."

"Yes, DOCTOR Robert Bower," he replied emphasizing his doctoral title, "the university's newest associate professor of business ethics. And, I'm pleased to meet Elizabeth's roommate."

"Elizabeth?" I questioned. Whoa. Liz never let anyone call her that... other than her own mother. I only dared call her Elizabeth if I wanted to pick a fight. She and I had an understanding. She never called me Kristen and I never called her Elizabeth. This made me wonder about Dr. Bower.

"Robert insists on calling me Elizabeth. Isn't that sweet?" she gushed, as Robert held the door open for her.

"This is worse than I thought!" was the look I gave her as Robert closed the door behind them. That quickly, they were gone. I was left gawking at the door.

Between my hours at the Psychology Department office, the campus bookstore, and tutoring, I didn't spend much time with Robert and Liz. Liz, however, had all the time in the world to spend with Robert. He was the reason she quit waiting tables at the diner, turned in her apron, and donated her ghastly gold dress to the Salvation Army. Instead of waiting on customers at the diner, she waited on Robert. They picnicked, strolled around the campus lake, and went to all the summer recitals. He bought her flowers, clothes, and jewelry. He charmed her with gifts, and only expected all of her time in return. When Robert had a class or a department meeting, Liz lost herself in a practice room and played the piano by the hour. When Robert wasn't teaching or meeting, he expected Liz to be at his beck and call. Robert enjoyed nothing more than waltzing around campus, attending cocktail parties, and generally just being seen with his trophy on his arm. Liz was completely satisfied fulfilling that role. Soon after Labor Day, he began hinting toward a wedding and 'living happily ever after.' Liz was smitten, of that there was no doubt.

The doubt, though, stood in the form of Alistair Ashley... Liz's father. Liz was Ash Ashley's only daughter. She was his princess. He had spent her entire life paying for the absolute best for her. He invested in years of music lessons, private school, and dance classes. His wife, Beatrice, also known as Bea, spent a small fortune on clothes, shoes, and accessories for their daughter. Ash never regretted a penny spent for his sweet girl. In his mind, there was no one good enough to marry his Elizabeth. Convincing her father to see the good in Robert, and haggling with her mother over the wedding details, gave Liz and me one last year together in the attic apartment. A year spent planning a storybook wedding. Another gift.

"Mom! Please listen to me, I only want one attendant. Kris. No more!" Liz sat surrounded by fabric swatches, menu samples, copies of <u>*Brides*</u> *magazine, and a cup of tea. The first thing I noticed when I walked in was the tea. Liz only drank tea when she was stressed. Looking at the number of tea bags on the counter in*

the kitchen confirmed she had been on the phone for a long time.

"Mother," she groaned. "I don't care about proper etiquette, society protocol, or Emily Post. I will only have one bridesmaid, Kris. I think the simplicity of having just one attendant will be quite elegant."

The wedding became Liz's life. In fact, not only did she quit her job at the diner, she dropped her classes. As their only daughter, Ash and Bea Ashley, were determined to marry Liz off in a high society manner. Between time with Robert and phone calls with her mother, Liz's life didn't have room for much else.

"It's the first Friday of January, wanna go get pizza or have it delivered?" I asked.

"Mom," Liz interrupted her mother's monologue. "Mom, I have to go. I will look over the napkin swatches one more time and decide tomorrow. Bye."

"Phew! Thanks for the rescue, Friend!" sighed Liz.

I'm not sure when it had happened but we had both slipped into the comfortable habit of referring to each other as 'Friend.' Rarely, did we call each other by name.

"So, pizza?" I asked again over a knock at the door.

Somewhere along the way, Dan discovered our First Friday tradition. Before Liz could answer my question, I opened the door. Dan was standing on the threshold holding two pizza boxes and a bottle of wine.

"Dan, if I weren't already engaged, I'd marry you!" Liz shouted. "You're amazing!"

chapter 5

"And, I'm forever grateful that both of you were quick to recognize all my amazingness," Dan says, quietly walking into Liz's bedroom and slipping in next to me. With a quick squeeze of my shoulder, he leans over and gently kisses Liz's forehead. "How are you doing tonight, Lizzie?"

She opens her eyes and an entire conversation takes place in a moment's look between them. Theirs is a mutual admiration built on years of kindness, compassion, and lots of laughter. It is also an exclusive club. I've never been invited. I gave up any jealousy a long time ago.

"Mom," Mark's voice catches as he steps to Jenny's side of the bed. Holding Jenny's hand, he gently leans down and whispers in his mother's ear, "I've missed you, Mom. It's good to be home."

"Home," Liz croaks. "Soon."

"I love you much, Mom."

"Love. You."

"To the moon and back, Mom," tears pool in Mark's eyes, "to the moon and back."

Jenny leans into Mark, her protector. Just three years apart in age, Mark solemnly took on the role of Jenny's protector the day Liz brought Baby Jenny home from the hospital. When little Jenny woke up to find her daddy gone, she fell asleep in her big brother's bed for months. I used to marvel at the fact that Mark and Jenny never had sibling arguments.

"They're best friends," was Liz's only answer. "They learned early to cling to each other."

As I watch the exchange between Mark, Liz, and Jenny, tears stream down my cheeks. Saying goodbye is hard. How do children prepare for this? How does a mother say goodbye? How will we breathe without her?

"*Remember to count the gifts*," I hear her voice from conversations past. "*Even at the end, count... and count for me too*." Tonight is for her. Her gifts came home to give her one last gift. Sometimes counting the gifts is the gift itself.

I don't realize Luke's presence until he puts his hand on my arm. Standing, I hug him. My son, an Army chaplain like my father... a musician like his other mother. He belongs to both of us. In the silence of Liz's room, I realize that we all belong to each other. We are bound by a deep love and a deep history that centers around her. Together, we are her family.

"I've got coffee and tea ready in the kitchen, and the church auxiliary group dropped off a deli tray earlier," Jana says, stopping outside the bedroom door. Jana's the one with experience. She has done this before. Tonight, she is our leader and we deftly follow her to the kitchen.

"I can't do this," Jenny sobs. "Please, someone, please help her."

I search Jana's eyes for help, for wisdom, for the How-To manual to do this thing called death and grief.

"Jenny, if I may," Jana steps in wrapping her arms around Jenny's petite frame. "Honey, the absolute greatest gift you can give your mama tonight is to stay by her side. This is equally hard for her. She needs to be surrounded by those she loves and those who love her." Jenny nods into Jana's shoulder.

"I know this is the hardest thing you have ever done. It will also be the greatest thing. I promise that a day will come when you will look back on tonight and be thankful for this last night with your mom."

I marvel at Jana's wisdom. This night, tonight, is a gift.

"Love on her, Jenny, she needs you," Jana gently lets go of Jenny and hands her a box of tissues.

"Now," she says with authority, "I made a promise to your

mama." She looks around at the five of us gathered in Liz's kitchen.

"I made a promise to your Liz," she repeats. "I could not promise no tears, but I did promise no pity. She wants to celebrate this combined family tonight. Let's give her a celebration of your family... her life. I, for one, would like to hear more of the story."

Jana's pep talk speaks to our hearts. We all smile at her reference to "your Liz." Liz is ours... she belongs with all of us. With a collective deep breath and filled mugs of coffee, tea, and even hot cocoa for Luke, we gather around our Liz. Jenny and Luke sit on either side of her and Mark sits at her feet. The rest of us pull chairs close and listen to the November rain on the window pane.

Gathering my thoughts is becoming more and more difficult. I cannot remember where I am in this story... our story. In a matter of seconds, a myriad of memories flood my mind, all jumbled.

"You were at the wedding," Dan reaches for my hand.

"Theirs or ours?" I question.

"Both."

~*~

"When are you going to wake up and see the treasure standing right in front of you?" Liz asked me one night while I

brushed my teeth.

"Wah?" I mumbled as I brushed.

"Darlin', Dan is one hundred percent prime-time in love with you!" she giggled.

"Serious? Dan? Me?! No. Way."

"Uh. Huh," she looked at me. "Wait a minute... are you telling me this is a mutual feeling?"

"Oh Liz! I'm crazy about him, but I've always thought he was still interested in you," I wailed. "I don't stand a chance."

"I can't believe this!" Liz screamed. She started dancing around the room singing, "Matchmaker, matchmaker, make me a match. Find me a find. Catch me a catch...."

Liz loved the Fiddler on the Roof *musical. She would often randomly sing the songs from the show. I had no idea, though, that while she was singing, she was conniving.*

"We need a plan," she announced. "Hmmm, what we can do?"

Liz liked to have a plan for everything. She wanted to stay up all night creating a fool-proof plan to get Dan and me together. She tried to talk me into a late night planning session. I was exhausted. The only plan I wanted to be part of was a plan for a good night's sleep. Had I been willing to stay up with her, we might have had a fool-proof plan. Instead, I left it up to her and went to bed. Liz came up with a plan on her own. It equalled a disaster... and another gift.

"Dan, would you mind helping us move a new couch up to the apartment?" Liz asked over the phone.

"You can come at 6? Great! We appreciate this SO much," she gushed. "Of course, we will feed you. See you then."

I shot her daggers. She lied to one of her best friends. There was no new couch. Her lame plan, though, included lying to Dan to get him to come over. As soon as he came in, she would "remember" that Robert's class was finished and they had a party to go to. The plan was lame, but that wasn't the worst part about it. Liz left it up to me to explain to Dan that there was no couch and then to treat him to dinner instead. She even pressed a twenty into my hand when she hung up the phone.

Needless to say, the entire evening was a disaster. I explained the lack of a couch to Dan as we walked to Village Pizza and waited forty minutes for a table. When we finally squeezed into the smallest booth they had, we had to continue to wait. In the end, we waited over ninety minutes to eat mediocre pizza with burnt cheese and pepperoni. The pizza was so bad, even Dan didn't want to take home what was left. After I awkwardly explained Liz's antics, there was nothing left to say. I paid with Liz's money and we walked home. The evening felt like a fiasco. However, if Liz's plan was just to get Dan and me together, the plan worked beautifully. On the walk home from an awkward and pathetic dinner, Dan took my hand and said, "I'm glad Liz did this for us." He always did understand her better than I.

For a few weeks, Liz gloated over her matchmaking victory. It didn't take long, though, before she poured her energies into planning not just one wedding... two. She would leave pictures of wedding dresses on my dresser, pamphlets for reception facilities, and lists of florists on our table. The bathroom mirror sported yellow sticky notes reminding me to call a photographer, look at the pamphlets on the table, and decide how many attendants I wanted to have.

Overwhelmed, I simply ignored her efforts. Instead of giving in to an anxiety attack, I just walked away from Liz's wedding suggestions. When Liz continued to hound me and I could take it no longer, I locked myself in my room and opened my art box. When she realized she wasn't going to get anywhere with me, Liz turned to Dan. After a brief conversation with him, I wisely turned my wedding planning over to both of them. It was perfect. Liz loved surprises. And, Dan loved nothing better than to surprise me. I often caught them whispering and giggling. I pretended not to notice. My only request was that our wedding not take place while Robert and Liz honey-mooned in Italy.

Liz not only put her foot down about having just one bridal attendant, she also insisted that Colonel and Mom Murphy make it to her wedding.... as if they would disagree. My parents were under her spell just like the rest of us. Liz and my mom spent an entire week on the phone calling back and forth to arrange schedules, flight times, car rental, and lodging. Liz paid for it all. How she convinced Colonel Murph to let her pay, I will never know. The fact that he agreed, though, is another gift.

As soon as graduation was over and Robert's office was locked for the summer, the four of us traveled to the Ashley Estate for the wedding week. My parents arrived shortly after. Bea Ashley had the entire week planned out for us. She scheduled a bridal shower luncheon, threw a bachelorette breakfast, and had the bachelor dinner catered. She arranged various garden parties, photography sittings, and cocktail parties. There were distant relatives to meet and society to greet. All to be done before Liz walked down the aisle. As always, Liz played the part of graceful bride and thoughtful daughter perfectly. I played a brilliant role as the quiet bridal attendant. Once again, I had no idea the tricks up Liz's sleeve.

Friday morning, I opened my eyes to see a note and a white rose lying on the pillow next to me. When I sat up to read the note, I saw the most beautiful cream and antique lace dress hanging on my closet door.

I don't want to wake one more morning without you. Would you meet me for breakfast in the gazebo? All my love, Dan

Even though she loves surprises, Liz can hardly keep a secret.

Before I could get out of bed, she poked her head in my room grinning from ear to ear. Without saying a word, she ushered me to the bathroom, opened the shower door for me to step into, and walked out. When I finished in the bathroom, Liz was dressed and ready to go. She wore a gorgeous coral-colored lawn dress with matching nail polish on her toes. Painting my toes to match, she soon had me dressed with my hair done and my makeup perfect. Even better, we walked barefoot across the early morning dew-covered grass. I have always hated wearing shoes.

"How?" I finally asked, not sure if I wanted to know the details. Knowing, though, that I did not want to be in the dark any longer.

"All details will be explained by Dan, later," she grinned. "I will tell you that I designed your dress. Since Janet, my seamstress, already had your measurements for the dress for my wedding, she was able to make this dress for you."

"Liz!" I squealed. "Really! Really, Friend, this is too much!"

"You get what you get and you don't throw a fit," she answered laughing. "Please, let me do this. Honestly, the dress is really all I did. My parents are providing breakfast and Dan did the rest. Ask no more questions until later, or you will ruin your day."

Standing on the lawn under the morning sun, I hugged her and we wiped each other's eyes. Then we picked up our skirts and ran the rest of the way to the gazebo. Liz opened the screen door and I walked into a fairy land of little lights, antique lace, and the love of my life standing with Robert, my parents, Liz's parents, and a minister. As the colors of the sunrise painted the sky, Dan and I pledged our lives to each other. Over the most elaborate breakfast I had ever seen, we celebrated with those we loved most. Liz's photographer captured my moment. I danced barefoot to Liz's accompaniment on the harp. For the moment, I lived my own fairy tale. The two I loved most planned a wedding for me that could not have been more perfect.

Later, that same day, while the sunset colored the sky canvas in reds, yellows, oranges, and magentas, guests gathered in an enormous tent on the south lawn of the Ashley Estate. With the brilliant sunset reflecting off the outside of the huge white tent, little white lights and candles lit the inside. Among lace and flowers, friends, and family, Liz's fairy tale wedding took place. Dressed in a sapphire floor-length silk dress and matching shoes, I held Liz's bouquet and adjusted her long lace train. In her white silk Cinderella gown, she vowed to love, honor, and cherish Robert until parted by death. With seven hundred and fifty of their closest friends and family, the two became Dr. and Mrs. Robert Andrew Bower. Two fairy tale weddings in one day. Two best friends in love.

The party waned in the early morning hours. After Ash and

Bea sent Dr. and Mrs. Robert Bower off for Italy, they handed us the key to their guest house. Liz's last wedding gift to us was a stocked pantry and full refrigerator. There was no need to go anywhere, so Dan and I locked ourselves in. We didn't come out for a week. I spent the week asking Dan a thousand questions about all the details of our fairy tale wedding. He spent the week answering each and every one. Liz's wedding week... my wedding week... became a week of a thousand gifts and more.

The greatest gift of all... Dan.

chapter 6

I pause and lose myself in the remembering. My mind floods with memories I have hidden in my heart and cherished for twenty-four years. Memories that are Dan's and mine alone. Lost in his own memories, he reaches for my hand.

“Were you ever sorry your family wasn't there?” Jenny asks Dan.

“At the time, I was,” Dan replies quietly. “I called my mom to let her know that I was getting married and that I would find a way to pay for their trip, if she and my dad would come. She said she'd see about it. I knew that was her way of evading the issue. She said she wished me luck and that my dad would be home soon. She said 'good-bye' and hung up. The entire phone conversation lasted about three minutes. It was the last time I spoke with my mom.”

"Three years later, a neighbor sent Dan the newspaper clipping at his university address. For a reason only God can understand, Stan and Doris McClintock were killed in a car accident by a drunk driver," I finish.

"I'm sorry I asked, Uncle Dan," Jenny apologizes.

"Jenny," Dan smiles, "it's okay. I don't talk about my parents much because I don't know what to say. My greatest goal in life has been to be a better dad than the father I had."

"Have you eaten?" he whispers, changing the subject, though he knows the answer.

"Mmm... lunch... maybe," I mumble.

"Come on," he leads me to my feet.

Luke, Dan, and I make our way to the kitchen counter, where Jana had the church auxiliary ladies' deli tray laid out with a loaf of her own homemade bread.

"Mmm... Jana, you spoil us," Luke gushes, piling turkey and ham high onto a slice of Jana's bread. "I, for one, am grateful for your bread. It's a gift!" He chuckles at his own joke.

"It really is my pleasure," Jana replies. "I don't usually make bread for the families of my patients. Your family is special, though. I wish I hadn't met you under these circumstances, but I am grateful for your influence in my life. Through knowing you, I'm learning to open my heart to see the gifts all around me and to be grateful for them. Thank you all for teaching me to live a life of gratitude."

"Thank you for sharing, Jana," Dan smiles. "I think that is the most I have ever heard you say."

"It is," she quietly replies. "I'm glad I got a chance to tell you, though."

Gathering with our small supper around Liz's kitchen table, Jana shares some of her gratitude list. We look at pictures of her granddaughters and laugh at their antics. In that very moment, Jana shares a gift with me. As I hear her proudly talk about her own children, grandchildren, and especially the new little one on the way, I realize that life and death, joy and sorrow, healing and pain all coexist in this journey called life. And, it is okay that they do.

"Jana, thank you for caring for Liz. Thank you for sharing your list with us. And, thank you for showing me there is joy in the pain," I hug her. We both wipe our leaky eyes.

"Can I hear more of the story?" she asks. "Or, do we need to wait for Jenny and Mark?"

"They know this story better than I do," I laugh. "They just like to hear me talk."

~*~

"Thank you!" I hugged Bea Ashley at the end of honeymoon

week. "Thank you for everything!"

"You are so welcome, dear!" She embraced me. "You have been such a good friend to Elizabeth."

"Thank you, too, sir," I put my hand out to shake Ash's hand.

"It's certainly time for you to stop calling me 'sir,' and to give me a hug," he chuckled swallowing me in a big bear hug.

Part of the details that Dan and Liz worked out, before the weddings, was the return of Robert's sedan. When Robert and Liz left for their Italian honeymoon, Robert handed his car keys to Dan. Dan and I used our second week of vacation to drive Robert's car back to the university. We pulled out of the Ashley's Estate waving good-bye to Ash and Bea.

Rather than hurry back to the rat race of life, we took that week to savor time, wander country roads, and find quaint Bed and Breakfast Inns. By the time we arrived at the apartment, Robert's car was overflowing with treasures we had unearthed at obscure antique stores.

"I'll go unlock the door and be right down to help you carry the steamer trunk up," I said, getting out of the car.

"Just unlock the door and hold it open. I'll carry it up," Dan said, opening the back door to the sedan.

When Dan got to the top of the stairs with the trunk, he found me standing in the kitchen with tears running down my face. Everywhere I looked were signs that Liz was gone. While we enjoyed the extra week driving back, she and Robert returned from Italy and moved her things into his apartment. She and I no longer shared the sweet little attic apartment. Though I was thrilled to be the one to keep the apartment, and even more excited to be Mrs. Dan McClintock, I missed my friend. Setting the steamer trunk on the kitchen floor, Dan enveloped me in his arms.

"Let's unload and make this our apartment," he said, wiping the tears from my cheeks. "Then we'll invite Robert and Liz over to see the transformation."

We should have known that Liz would not wait that long. Before the last basket was unloaded and our suitcases were carried up, Liz and Robert walked up the street. Laughing, talking, and interrupting each other, we got everything into the apartment. We had been apart for two weeks. The first two weeks of our new lives. Liz and I hardly took a breath. Dan and Robert gave up trying to keep up and went out for Chinese carry-out. When they returned, Liz finished setting the last piece in place. She did her magic again. The apartment was perfect. From that night forth, Liz has been my sole interior decorator. She knows how to make a home.

I spent the remainder of the summer looking for a permanent social work job. At each interview, I heard the same thing, "We'd love to hire you. However, we need to fill the Affirmative Action quotas. If you were a male or a minority, we would hire you right now. You are perfectly qualified. I'm sorry. We will have to pass on you."

At the end of summer, Dan started medical school and I felt discouraged and defeated. In a desperate attempt for a job, I wandered into the diner and walked out with my own gold double-breasted dress. Liz laughed. I continued to hope and pray for something else.

Though I never enjoyed it the way Liz did, the job at the diner paid the rent and put food on our table. I found some of the diners to be interesting and others to be a little strange. For their part, the diners loved me, only because they had first loved my friend, Liz. Despite the fact that wearing the gold dress was awful, the job at the diner wasn't.

Liz and I talked every day. Dan and I were happy. Life was good. The only cloud on the horizon was Robert's mood swings. Liz would excuse his moodiness to stress. We were too naïve to disagree. Eventually, it seemed, he would come around and he would laugh with us again. We were too young to recognize the gifts all around us, and too happy to think life would ever be any different.

chapter 7

Walking back into Liz's room, we see Jenny curled up on the bed next to her mother.

“How's she doing?” Dan whispers to Mark.

“Her breathing sounds the same, but she's no longer responding to our voices,” Mark whispers back. “I guess she's asleep.”

“Is Jenny sleeping?”

“No,” she says quietly. “I don't want to sleep. I just want to absorb all of this. Seeing her lying next to me, listening to her breathe, smelling her perfume on this pillow... I want all of this and more.”

Dan takes my place on the other side of Liz. I take the chair again.

“Ah, Lizzie,” he says, smoothing her top blanket. “You've

gifted us much."

In those few words, Dan conveys what we all feel. Liz touched us each differently... she is a kindred spirit, loving mother, lifelong friend, cancer patient. And, to each of us, she is a gift of grace.

"Does it hurt her to have me laying here?" Jenny asks Jana.

"Don't worry, she'll let us know if she's hurting," Jana replies. "Stay there as long as you'd like."

"Jana, how do you do this over and over and over again," Mark quietly asks. "How do you know exactly what to do, what to say?"

"I don't know exactly," Jana replies. "I only know what I've learned from these years of home health care. It's a hard job. It's families like yours that keep me going, though. Maybe Luke has a better answer."

"I agree, sitting by one dying is hard," Luke replies. "There were times in Afghanistan that I wanted to quit and come home. You see things no one should see. You hear things no one should hear. But, in the end, you sit by the next dying person hoping that in their last few minutes you might be able to make a difference."

"Exactly," Jana nods.

"Jana, you're making a difference," Mark smiles. "Thanks for being with us."

"You know, Mark," Dan starts, "I remember an illustration

that I heard a Protestant minister share that might help us understand tonight a little bit better. My friend, Reverend Paul Rogers, shared with me the illustration that our life on earth is like our spiritual gestational time. When the time comes for us to take our last earthly breath, it is as if we are then birthed to heaven to spend all of eternity in God's presence. I was not there when you were born, Mark. However, I have assisted in many births in my career. Rarely are they calm and peaceful. Most births include a lot of turmoil and travail when the baby enters this world. Often, the same is true when it comes time for us to leave this world. Death is sometimes a long ordeal with its own turmoil and travail. However, when we leave this world, those of us who know Christ as our Savior are birthed into eternal life with Him. It's this kind of eternal perspective that makes it worth it."

"I like that thought," Mark smiles. "Thanks for sharing it. It doesn't take away the pain of watching Mom suffer, but it does give me some eternal perspective."

"I was there the night you were born, Mark. I promise you, there was plenty of turmoil and travail. You gave your mom fits that night," I chuckle. "We didn't think you were ever going to get here."

~*~

"Kris!" Liz squealed into the phone. "I am meeting you at the coffee shop! I have two incredible things to tell you."

"I won't be off work for another twenty-five minutes, Liz. Want to meet me at the apartment in a half hour? Dan has a late lab tonight."

"Sure and I'll bring the coffee!"

Thirty minutes later, Liz knocked once and walked right in with two flavored coffees, almond roca for her and French vanilla for me.

"Where are you?" she hollered.

"In the shower. Give me five minutes."

"Hurry!" Patience was not one of Liz's fine qualities. I came out four minutes later in my flannel pajamas with a towel wrapped around my head.

"Mmmm... is this decaf?" I asked, taking my first sip.

"Of course, it's 9 p.m." she replied.

"So, what's so important that I had to shave a minute off of my shower?" I asked savoring the sweet vanilla latte.

"I have found your dream job," she announced.

"Really?" I replied, ever the skeptic.

"Yes, really! You know Barb Wilson, right?" I shook my head as I took another sip.

"Well, I thought you knew her through Anna Manns and Julie Stevenson. Anyway, she is the secretary to Dr. Helen McIntyre,

head of the art department. I ran into her today when I went to campus to use a practice room in the music building," Liz stopped to take a sip of her almond roca.

I waited. Sometimes Liz liked to draw a story out by adding dramatic flair. I guess I learned a while ago that if I didn't acknowledge her dramatic pause, she would continue the story faster. I took another sip and just looked at her.

"You know, I hate it when you don't play along," she huffed. "Anyway, she mentioned that Dr. McIntyre has a new art theory manuscript and she's looking for someone to illustrate the cover."

"Serious?" I asked.

"Of course I'm serious! I tease you about a lot of things. Never your art."

"You're right, you don't. So what else did she tell you?"

"She said if you, Kris Murphy McClintock, are interested, then you should go see Dr. McIntyre tomorrow."

"Tomorrow," I whispered. Suddenly my heart raced and my stomach churned. My art had always been a private thing for me. It was all I could do to enter a few art contests in high school. All the time I had been at the university, I had never pursued an art class or contest. It scared me half to death to consider using my art for income.

"What if she doesn't like my style, my works?" I asked meekly.

"What if she does," she smiled. "You won't know if you don't

try."

"I'll think about it and talk to Dan about it."

"Promise to call me the minute you walk out of her office," she insisted.

"What makes you think I will go?" I replied, starting to feel my heart rate returning to normal.

"Because you are gifted," Liz answered, without hesitation.

"Ok, so what's the second thing?" I asked.

"Second thing?" she giggled, pretending she didn't know what I was talking about.

I took another sip of my coffee and savored it. I was tired from work. I was now stressing a little about letting Dr. McIntyre see my art work and Liz was trying to be sly. Once again, I just sat there and enjoyed my coffee. I didn't have to wait long.

"You are no fun, you know that?" She whined.

"If that were true, you wouldn't be here," I quipped. "So, what's number two?"

"Well...." she tried one more dramatic pause and when I didn't jump in, she shouted, "we're pregnant!!!"

Apparently she does know how to get a reaction from me. I jumped up, spilled my coffee, and screamed. Dan walked in to Liz and me jumping around the apartment dancing, screaming, and crying.

"Woo hoo! Yeah!" he shouted, jumping right into the

celebration. Then he looked at us and said, "What are we hollering about?"

"We're pregnant!" We both shouted. At Dan's shocked facial expression, I quickly adjusted my words. "They're pregnant... Robert and Liz are having a baby!!"

"Woo hoo!" he said again, whirling us around the room.

Liz's excitement lasted throughout the days and weeks of extreme morning sickness. Still madly in love with Robert, she couldn't wait to have his baby. As the months progressed and her belly grew, her heart swelled more.

"I just can't wait to see this baby. I love her so much, sometimes I feel like my heart will burst with love!" She confided one day.

"Her?" I asked.

"Her. Him. I don't care. I just want to be a mom!" she answered.

"Better you than me," I replied.

"So, as I sit here incubating," she said, stretching out on my well worn couch, "tell me what they thought of the cookbook cover?"

"They loved it. No editing, no improvements, no do-over. I guess I am officially a freelance artist," I sighed. "And, it feels good... really, really good.... to be done at the diner."

"All because you listened to me and went to see Dr.

McIntyre," she gloated.

"Yes, you are so wise and so right," I answered. "So glad you know me well enough to know when to push me beyond myself."

"That's what I'm here for," she said. "You know, this pregnancy stuff is incredible. You should try it!"

"No," I quickly responded. "We've just started medical school. There's school and his residency... it will be a while. End of discussion."

"You just said you liked it when I push you beyond yourself," Liz chided.

"Enough. Just enjoy your pregnancy for both of us," I huffed.

"That's easy," she answered. "I already do."

On the days that Robert and Dan were busy on campus, Liz and I shopped for the baby. I had no idea how many baby things there were and how much a tiny baby needed. According to Liz, her baby needed it all. The two things that saved Robert from being buried alive in baby paraphernalia was Liz's discriminatory taste and the diminutive size of their apartment.

Liz was always beautiful. As an expectant mom, though, she was exquisite. By the end of her pregnancy she had only gained eighteen pounds. Her basketball shaped belly stretched far out in front of her. Ever the fashionista, Liz had developed her own maternity style. She never looked lovelier than she did in a mu-mu with a scarf draped around her swollen belly and Birkenstocks on her swollen feet.

Liz made me promise to be with her during labor and delivery. I attempted to talk her out of this absurd thought about a million times. At one point, I even tried to talk her into having Dan be with her, instead of me.

"Why would I want Dan there?" she asked one day. "You. You will be there. You will be my doula."

"Doula?!? What the heck is a doula and why do I have to be yours?" I responded.

"A doula is one who helps the mother as she gives birth. The doula encourages the mother, gets things for her, and generally keeps the mother calm and happy. Then, when the baby enters this world, he or she enters a calm and peaceful atmosphere with a very happy mama," she recited from a website she had found on childbirth.

"Seriously? I think you just want an excuse to make me your slave for the day."

"That too!" She giggled.

The night Robert called me, I had just fallen asleep. I was sick. I was worn out. A flu bug had hit hard and fast. For two days I could keep nothing down.

"I'm sorry, Robert. I'm sick," I croaked into the phone.

"She's just going to have to do this without me."

"She says she needs you. She says, if you don't come, she will have this baby in your living room. I'm sorry you don't feel well. Seriously Kris, she's not really in a compromising mood right now. Would you please come and be here, just for a little while?" he pleaded. I was never good at saying 'no' to Liz.

I'm not sure what I expected Liz's birth experience to be like. I am, however, quite confident I did not expect it to include screaming and gnashing of teeth! Sixteen long hours of whining, yelling, crying, and screaming. When I wasn't rubbing her shoulders, feeding her crushed ice, cooling the cloth for her forehead, and holding her hand, I sat in awe at how demanding my friend had become. I had no idea Liz had it in her. It was as if she had an alter personality. At the end of the travail, though, she calmly and gracefully held her newborn son.

"His name is Mark Andrew," she proudly announced when Dan arrived. "And he will be best friends with your little one."

"WHAT?!" I shouted

"You're pregnant, which is why you've been sick," she giggled, confidently.

"No! Way!" I said.

"Hmmm..," Dan mused, as a look of understanding passed between him and Liz.

"I'm not having this conversation with you two," I answered.

Seven months later, we had the conversation as Luke Murphy quietly entered this world. Holding my hand, feeding me ice chips, and rubbing my shoulders, Liz gloated. With each contraction she would remind me that she was the first one to know that Luke was on his way. And, with each contraction, I would say, "Shut up, Liz!" However, there was nothing I could say to deter her from her moment. Even though I was the one giving birth, it was as much Liz's moment, as mine or Dan's.

"Did it bother you that Liz was here for his birth," I asked Dan later.

"Are you kidding?" he answered, rocking Luke. "She was the entertainment. What would we do without her?"

"I agree," I replied. "I hate it, though, when she's right and she gloats."

More gifts... Mark, Luke, and the relationship between my two best friends.

chapter 8

“Do you mind if I join you,” Mike asks, softly.

“Mike!” Jenny whispers, gently jumping up from the bed to kiss her fiance.

“Hey Mike!” Mark steps over to shake his hand. “It's good to see you again.”

“You too, Mark,” Mike says, hugging Jenny.

“Are you hungry?” Jenny asks. “The church ladies brought some sandwich stuff.”

“Sounds good,” Mike replies, gently. “How's California been, Mark?”

“It's been good. If you don't mind if I join you, I'll fill you in on all that has been going on,” Mark answers.

“I'm sorry if I sound inconsiderate. I'm starved. We assisted with a car accident at 11:30 this morning and then had a barn fire at 4 p.m. I haven't had much to eat today. Do you mind if I eat while you talk?" Mike asks, walking out with Mark and Jenny.

"How are you doing?" Dan asks me, while watching the younger people walk out.

Again, I don't answer right away. How do I put into words these emotions in my heart? I don't know how to say all that I feel. I don't know how to articulate the pain. I don't know where to find the words that equally express my gratitude for our twenty-eight years together and the anger I feel that I can't have twenty-eight more. I reach for Dan's hand, again. I can't find an answer to his question, so I say nothing.

Dan stands up from the side of Liz's bed and pulls me up to him. There, standing next to the best friend that we share, he encircles me with his strong arms. These are the same arms that have held our babies, carried our sleeping children, and moved furniture many times at Liz's whims. As he holds me, I remember the many nights his arms held me as I cried in anticipation of this. I soak his shirt with my tears before I realize I'm crying again. I am that numb. Dan says nothing.

"Just hold me," I sniff. "And, please don't let go."

I feel his arms loosen around me. As I look up to him in surprise and shock for letting go. He smiles and sits back down in the recliner next to the bed pulling me to him. The two of us barely fit.

“I'm glad you are not too old for that,” Luke smiles at us.

I can only imagine what we look like from his vantage point. Two old people with arms and legs at all angles hanging off a recliner built for one. I doubt we look graceful. I know we still look very much in love.

“Thank you for teaching me much about marriage. I look at you two and I know it will be worth it to wait for the right girl,” Luke says softly. Luke doesn't talk much about his relationships and I stopped asking a long time ago. God and I, though, talk about it often.

“Marriage is hard, Son,” Dan replies. “You often get out of it what you put into it. If you invest wisely, you will be blessed beyond measure.”

“I think Aunt Liz taught me more about marriage than you did,” Luke mutters, softly.

“Don't forget,” Dan answers. “Marriage is a partnership. When one partner abdicates, the other partner can't force them to stay in the relationship. The only way a great marriage works is if both partners give one hundred percent.”

“Liz did the best she could with what she had,” I whisper. “He wasn't much to work with.”

“I know,” Luke says quietly. “Last year when Aunt Liz took me out for my birthday, she told me more about Robert. I just don't get why he never loved, honored, or cherished her.”

Liz has always been Aunt Liz to my kids, just as I am Aunt Kris to hers. Dan is Uncle Dan. Robert, however, is just plain Robert. Children have an uncanny ability to see thorough a situation to the heart of the matter. From the time they were little, my kids never wanted to give Robert the loving title of Uncle. They recognized the proverbial wolf in sheep's clothing. Luke and Ryan released early what it took Liz a long time to see.... that sometimes what you see isn't what you get.

~*~

"So, how's Robert these days. It seems like forever since we've seen him," I asked Liz one beautiful day, as we pushed our strollers around the campus lake.

"Fine," came the vague reply.

"'Fine is the same answer you've given me every time I've asked since Mark was born," I stopped and looked at her. "What's going on, Liz?"

For a moment, Liz looked everywhere but at me. When she finally did answer my question, she avoided any eye contact. "Robert's just having a hard time adjusting to having a baby in the house," she replied.

"For goodness sake!" I huffed. "Mark will be one next month. Hasn't he had enough time to adjust by now?"

"Well, Mark doesn't sleep through the night yet. You know, it's hard when he's crying and won't sleep. Robert's responsibilities in the business department have increased. The head of the department gave him two new classes to teach, and he's now in an advisory position," she mumbled.

Liz finally looked in my eyes and started walking again. I knew that look. I had seen it before. Without saying a word, Liz plainly communicated that the topic of her and Robert was off limits. Pushing Luke alongside Mark's stroller, I knew eventually she would tell me all. Sometimes eventually comes sooner than you think.

"Look, Marky, it's Daddy," Liz crooned. "He must have seen us and is coming to meet us."

I looked up and saw Robert about fifty yards ahead of us coming out from the grove of trees. Before I could respond to Liz, I saw the obvious. Robert leaned down and kissed a young college student at a picnic table. It was even more obvious that he neither saw us, nor was he coming to meet up with Liz and Mark.

Someday I hoped to develop the moxie that came naturally to Liz. Instead of tucking tail and turning for home, Liz addressed the matter head on.

"Robert! Daddy!" Liz shouted, quickly pushing Mark's stroller toward the offending pair. "Look, Mark, Daddy's here."

Not wanting to miss a moment of this drama unfold, I opted to stand by the nearest tree to watch. I parked Luke's stroller in the shade and watched my friend star in an Emmy winning extemporaneous role.

"Isn't it a beautiful day, Robert? I'm so glad Mark and I got a chance to see you before we finished our walk," Liz beamed, as she reached the picnic table. "Oh, you have company? Hello, dear, who are you?"

Robert leaned in and whispered something to his companion.

"Oh, don't leave on my account," Liz said to the young girl that hurried away from the table. "I'm just here to say 'hi' to my husband and little Mark, here, wants to see his daddy. Hello, Sweetheart!" Liz planted a huge wet kiss on Robert's cheek.

"Elizabeth," Robert started to say. "I can explain...."

"Stop, Robert!" Liz hissed, as soon as the offending girl was gone. "Do not even try to explain this. Not only did I see you lean in and kiss that 12-year-old looking girl, so did Kris. She's standing over there."

Robert turned around and I gave him a little wave. Obviously, this would do nothing to endear me to him. It was certainly entertaining to watch. I was thoroughly enjoying the show. Robert didn't smile or wave back. Apparently, it wasn't very enjoyable to him.

"We'll talk later, Robert," Liz continued, allowing her voice to return to a normal volume. "Have a nice day!"

Liz turned Mark's stroller around and began retracing her steps toward me. Robert didn't move. As I watched him, standing motionless, staring at the ground, I almost felt sorry for him. Almost. When my friend made her way to me with tears filling her eyes, I did feel sorry. For her. In that moment, my opinion of Robert was considerably lower than my opinion of the scum that had settled on the bottom of the campus lake.

"Is he still there?" she asked tentatively, choking back the tears.

"Yep," I quietly replied. "Don't look back. He's not worth it."

"No, he's not," she answered. "But, he is Mark's father, and he is still my husband. I will have to deal with this sometime."

"Maybe he won't come home," I said, secretly wishing the easy way out for her.

"Oh, he'll be home," she began walking again. "He'll come home for dinner tonight with flowers and chocolate."

"Liz," I hesitated. "Has this happened before?"

"Yes and no," she replied. "Yes, he's been unfaithful. No, I've never seen him with that particular girl."

"Oh, Liz," I moaned. "I'm so sorry!"

"Don't be. I made my choice when I fell in love with him," she wiped her eyes. "Fortunately, my father didn't believe in marrying for love. He forced a prenuptial agreement. If Robert

leaves me for any reason, he gets nothing. Nada. Zip."

"I knew there was a reason I liked Ash Ashley," I laughed. I didn't say anything else as we walked. There was nothing left to say.

Later that night, lying in the dark, I told Dan about our walk around the campus lake. He listened quietly as I recounted all the details of Robert's unfaithfulness and Liz's brilliant performance.

"Her name is Amy," he said, when I finished.

"What?!" I sat up turning on the bedside lamp. "You know about this?"

"Yes," he replied. "And, I know about Maggie, Rachel, and Lynne. I'm sure there are others."

"How do you know all this?" I asked incredulously turning the light off again.

"Robert and his escapades are becoming well-known on campus," he said, wrapping me in his arms.

"And, the wife," I mused, "is always the last to know."

chapter 9

I climb out of the shared recliner, taking the spot on the bed next to Liz.

"I'm sorry the fairy tale was so short, Liz," I say, smoothing her peach-fuzz hair that has just recently began to grow again. "I hate that Prince Charming turned out to be such an ugly toad!"

"Hey, that's Mom's joke," Mark says.

"When did you come back in here?" I ask quietly, my hand still on Liz's head.

"Oh, around the point in the story when you were watching from the tree. I've always wondered why you never went with her for moral support?" he asks me.

"She didn't need me," I answer. "Your mother knew how to handle herself. She also knew how to handle your father."

"She sure did!" Dan chuckles. "Robert met his match in

Lizzie. You know, she became a legend among the faculty wives. She put up with a lot from him. She also demanded a lot. When it came right down to it, he paid mightily."

"He never paid anything," Mark grumbles. "All he did was lose access to Mom's money. He got away with it. He walked away. He never even paid child support."

I hear the hurt in his voice. Years of smothered pain surfaces. I turn from Liz to see the anger, bitterness, and pain in Mark's eyes.

"Your dad paid the highest price, Mark," I say. "He lost your mom, you, and Jenny. Don't give him more by allowing the bitterness and anger to eat at your heart."

Allowing Mark a few moments of solitude, I listen to Liz's breathing. I watch her chest rise and fall. I count her breaths and memorize the rhythm. Just as in all of life, the rhythm is changing. My own breath mimics her's. When her breathing catches, so does mine. I know I can't hold on to her much longer, but I don't know how to let go. The only thing I know how to do is to remember and to count. With each breath, I breathe "thank you... thank you... thank you...."

"Mark," Dan quietly answers, "Your mom had reason to be angry. There were times she was furious with Robert. She has not allowed her life to be defined by what Robert did or did not do. Liz became bitter once and her soul was almost consumed by it.

She refused to lose any more of her life to bitterness. She would often tell me that she gave Robert her heart once, and that she refused to lose any more of it by carrying a grudge."

"I continue to hate him, even after all the therapy," Mark replies angrily. "After all these years, I'm still angry."

"I know you are," Dan continues. "I was angry at Robert for a long time, myself. I pity him now."

"Why do you feel sorry for him?" Mark stammers. "He doesn't deserve your pity."

"I think he does," Dan looks deep into Mark's eyes as he continues. "I pity your father because I now see him as the weak man that he is. I used to be angry at who he was. I wanted to stand up and shout 'Get over yourself and be a man!' I was angry that he abdicated his marriage covenant with your mom for young college girls. I was livid that you and Jenny were left in his wake. I was bitter that he was spineless and weak. I resented that he seemingly got away with it. All of those emotions fermented in my soul until your mom intervened. It was she who showed me he should be pitied."

"Mom?" Mark asks. "How?"

"She told me that she pitied your father because he never knew you and Jenny. He never saw you grow up. I pity him, now, because he missed your Little League games. It moves me that he never heard Jenny's piano recitals or saw her play volleyball. I pity your father because he missed all your high school football games. When I watched you catch four touchdown passes in a single game, I felt sorry for your father. He was the one missing out. He's still the one missing out. I pity him that he doesn't know what an incredible man you've become. His own choices and actions have prohibited him from knowing two of the most incredible people on this earth... you and Jenny. My pity for him deepens because he doesn't know how great it is to be a father and a husband."

I look up to see Mark watching the rain on the window. Staring into the dark night, tears silently fall. The inner struggle of letting go of the years of anger, bitterness, and resentment show on his face.

"Mark," Dan continues, "you won't be able to let go of all of this tonight. Letting go is a process, a painful process. I know. I have spent all of my adult life letting go of the pain and bitterness my own father caused me. Trust me when I tell you that the freedom to pity Robert is worth the struggle. I'm not thankful for Robert's choices or for your pain. I am, however, deeply grateful that you allowed me to step into his shoes. Thank you for choosing me to fill his void. I've been honored to be your dad."

Dan stands to embrace Mark and I look at Liz. Nothing has

changed. Her eyes are still closed, her breathing still labored. I wonder how much she heard of Dan and Mark's conversation.

In the past, she's been most concerned with Mark. Even after he worked through his teenage rebellion, she knew he was still angry. So, she prayed. When Mark packed his Jeep with all of his earthly belongings and drove across the country, she prayed. When he settled in California with a software company, she prayed some more. When his calls home became less and less frequent, Liz prayed even more. She recognized the struggle in Mark's heart. Life has taught her that even a root of anger can eventually become a heart of bitterness. She knew peace could only come from surrendering that bitterness. She knew that freedom comes from forgiveness. She knew.

~*~

For a long time, Liz and I didn't discuss Robert's escapades. Honestly, there really was nothing to say. Liz threw herself into planning Mark's first birthday party. Though he neither recognized that it was his birthday nor cared about party favors, Liz would not let Mark's first birthday go unnoticed. She asked me to handcraft the invitations, place settings, and party favors all around the theme of A. A. Milne's classic, Winnie the Pooh. Liz took care of the coordinating, ordering, and decorating. When the time came, the party was perfect. Ash, Bea, Dan, Luke, and I gathered with Robert, Liz, and Mark to celebrate one year of Mark's life. After his perfunctory attendance, Robert left before the birthday cake was served. Though birthday party attendance is mandatory for every parent, no one complained when Robert disappeared. Liz relaxed and enjoyed her son, and Ash and Bea doted on Mark and Luke. It was the best first birthday party ever. A tradition was born. Liz chose the theme and planned the party. I handcrafted invitations and party favors. We made a great team!

Robert continued to pursue other women and Liz continued to stand by his side. Motherhood provided some sensational curves for Liz and she took every opportunity to capitalize on her new body. She attended every faculty and campus event as the doting wife on Robert's arm. She continued to play the role perfectly. At each event, she would spend the evening on Robert's arm looking gorgeous while making small talk. Women looked on with pity. They thought Robert's wife had no knowledge of her husband's shenanigans. Their men looked on with resentment what Robert was doing to Liz. At each event, Liz was completely aware of it all.

With each new girlfriend, real or rumored, Liz developed more bravery. Instead of buying a new cocktail dress off the rack of our local department store, Liz began designing her own dresses. She ordered fabric by the bolt and took the fabric and Mark for a long week at the Estate.

The first morning there, Liz met with her dressmaker, Janet. Liz and Janet had known each other for years. Liz attended elementary school with Janet's son, Brad. It was Janet who made all of Liz's high school formals and summer lawn party dresses. It was Janet who sewed Liz's wedding gown, as well as my dress, my bridesmaid dress, and Liz's dress for my wedding. Needless to say, it was Janet to whom Liz turned when she needed some new knockout gowns. Janet took Liz's new measurements and together they designed four gowns. By the end of the week, Liz went home with two of them, eager to show them off.

"Will you take Mark this Saturday?" Liz asked a few weeks later. "I'm done with student babysitters. It seems as if each new babysitter becomes a conquest for Robert."

"Even Megan?" I asked back.

"I don't know," she sighed. "According to the campus rumor mill, even Megan. I no longer know what is reality and what is rumor."

"It doesn't matter," I replied. "Of course, I will take Marky. What time?"

"Robert is insisting on dinner out before the summer faculty

recital. I think I should probably just put him down for his nap at your place. Is that okay?"

"It's great. He and Luke will have a great time together!"

Liz dropped Mark off for his nap and hurried home to get ready. She couldn't wait to wear one of her own dress designs. Apparently she did look gorgeous. When Robert saw her dressed and ready to go, he blew up. Though he had been unfaithful to her countless times, he could not abide by other men looking at his wife. Instead of dinner out, Robert lashed out at Liz in anger. For the first time, he roughed her up and forced himself on her. When he was finished physically, emotionally, and verbally exploiting his wife, he absolutely insisted that she put on the other new dress, redo her hair and makeup, and attend the recital on his arm. In that moment, the role that Liz had been playing became a nightmare.

To those attending the summer recital, nothing seemed amiss when Dr. and Mrs. Robert Bower found their seats. Liz looked radiant and Robert seemed attentive, for once. Looks are often deceiving. Only one person in attendance noticed that Robert seemed a little too attentive and Liz appeared a little too radiant. He watched and he wondered.

The summer faculty recital was the music department's semi-annual formal fundraiser. It was a brilliant performance done in two acts. The first act comprised of four professors each playing their own solo compositions. The trumpeter was amazing, as was the university's newest concert pianist. The cellist's piece moved the audience and the clarinetist performed an incredibly difficult piece flawlessly. For those few moments, Liz lost herself in the music. When the last soloist finished and the audience applauded, Liz realized Robert was gone.

Between the two music acts, black tie caterers silently mingled, serving hors d'oeuvres and cocktails. Still caught up in the brilliant musical performance, Liz reached for a flute of champagne. In her haste, she knocked the tray out of the server's hand. Before the server could react, the entire tray of champagne rained down on Liz. In one evening, Robert ruined one new gown and she managed to ruin the other. With tears and sputtered apologies, Liz turned to leave.

"Leaving so soon?" a gentle voice asked.

"Excuse me," Liz muttered, lowering her head and pushing past the voice. "Really, I must go."

"Would you like me to find Dr. Bower?" he asked. Liz looked up to a serene face and gentle eyes. She had once heard that the eyes are the windows to the soul. If so, she wondered if his soul was as beautiful as the two brilliant blue eyes that gazed at her with compassion, not pity.

"You know him?" she asked tentatively.

"Yes, he's a bit of a legend on campus," he said with a smile. Seeing the look on Liz's face, he quickly recanted. "I'm sorry, that was callous. I don't mean to make fun of your pain."

Liz looked at this man standing before her who seemed to truly be a gentleman. He wasn't as good looking or as charming as Robert. Instead, he had a sincerity and disposition that more than made up for his lack of fine features. In fact, his very presence was a study in contradiction. His gentle manner belonged at a recital, and his rugged looks seemed out of place wearing a tuxedo.

"No," Liz began, "please don't bother Robert. I'm sure he is previously occupied. I will just take a cab. I want to go home."

"Please, let me give you a ride. It will be faster than waiting for a cab on a Saturday night," he responded.

"No, really," Liz said, crying again. "I just want to go home."

"Come," he replied, calmly taking her hand. "I will take you. By the way, my name is Rob."

"Did you say 'Rob'?" she stammered.

"Yes," he smiled. "I have the dubious distinction of sharing a given name with your husband. However, I do prefer to be called 'Rob'."

"Okay," Liz acquiesced. Rob led her to the parking lot. Through her tears and stained dress, she did not see the eyes that followed them. Though none of the eyes belonged to Robert, she was still seen. Liz told me, much later, that she was confident that no one ever told Robert. Though she had never developed friendships with any of the other faculty wives, they gave her a gift that night. The gift of their silence.

After waiting up for Liz until after 2 a.m., I finally took myself to bed. I hoped she and Robert had a romantic evening, lost track of time, and were sleeping in. I didn't expect an early morning knock.

"Hi," Liz hesitated, as I opened the apartment door. "Is he awake?"

"No, it's a bit early, you know," I grumbled. I don't do mornings well. Especially the morning after my best friend didn't return for her son. "Where have you been?" I asked.

"I just lost track of time," she quietly replied. "I'll gather Mark's things and take him now."

"Want a cup of coffee first?" I asked.

"Sure."

"Where's Robert?" I wondered aloud, as I poured two cups of coffee.

"I'm not sure," she answered. I sat the two cups of coffee on

the table quietly. My friend who always looked pulled together was a disaster sitting in front of me. Sometimes I wished I knew how to probe people. This was definitely one of those times. The look on Liz's face, though, said that the topic was taboo. Liz finished her coffee. Without saying another word, she woke Mark and left.

Dan wandered out of our bedroom and saw me still at the table. Two empty coffee cups sat in front of me. He poured himself

what was left in the coffeepot and sat down.

"Where was she?" he asked. He had come home from his job at the hospital late and was surprised to see Mark's portable crib still in the living room.

"I don't know," I said softly. "I don't know."

Dan reached over and squeezed my hand and we both sat in the silence, wondering what had happened to our friend.

For a few weeks after that night, I tried to pretend all was the same, but Liz was different. For the first time in our friendship, she was the quiet, introverted one and I was the one trying to pull her out. I called often. I invited her for play dates, walks around the lake, shopping trips... really anything I could think of to reach out to her. Often she turned me down.

In a desperate attempt to reach my friend, I pushed Luke's stroller to her apartment one morning. I knocked on her door with chocolate in one hand and coffee in the other. When she opened the door, I gasped. She greeted me in stained and wrinkled pajamas, her hair in a tangled ponytail, and the apartment in a complete mess. In all the time we lived together, I had never seen her looking that badly.

"Hi," I said, holding up the chocolate and coffee. "I brought you something."

Liz glanced at me. Without a word, she walked away from the open door.

"Can we come in?" I asked. When she didn't answer, I awkwardly pushed Luke's stroller into her apartment balancing the coffee and chocolate. Mark squealed when he saw Luke. Soon the two of them were wrestling on the floor.

"Oooh, pretty!" I said, trying desperately to think of something to talk about. "What's in that box?"

An opened box sat on the floor with gorgeous fabric spilling out of it. Liz quietly got up and walked over to the box. Silently, she reached in and pulled out a spectacular silk gown of midnight blue with silver accents.

"I designed this for the department Christmas gala," she whispered.

"It's beautiful. I bet you can't wait to wear it," I replied, assuming that she would be attending the gala brilliantly

decorating Robert's arm.

"No," she answered. "I won't wear it. I will never wear it."

"What's going on?" I probed. "Are you okay?"

"I'm pregnant."

"Seriously!" I shrieked. "That's awesome!"

Liz, however, didn't seem to share my enthusiasm.

"Are you sick?"

"Very," she replied. "No offense, but that coffee smells horrible!"

The conversation quickly turned from the dress to Liz's condition. Though the moment ended in laughter, Liz did very little laughing over the next months. Even when the morning sickness subsided, my sunny-natured friend smiled little. Regardless of how often I would ask her what was wrong, she would always blame the pregnancy.

"I'm just tired," she would say. "Don't worry about me."

She said this, as if I could simply stop worrying. She wouldn't let me in. She chose to harbor her pain alone. So, I stood on the sidelines and worried about my friend. Liz had become a different person. I hardly recognized her. I felt as if I had lost my best friend. Actually, I felt as if I had lost them both. Dan had been sucked into the black hole called medical school. For the moment, he was no help. I watched Liz slip further and further away as her pregnancy progressed. Without Dan, I worried alone.

"What kind of man doesn't drive his wife to the hospital?" I grumbled, driving through the dark streets. Liz had called me between contractions. She asked to leave Mark with Dan and have me drive her to the hospital.

"The man who doesn't believe this child is his," she breathed through another contraction.

"He's pathetic," I mutter.

"He might be right," she said quietly, as I pulled into the hospital entrance.

A hospital volunteer greeted us with a wheelchair. Before I could question Liz about her response, she was gone around the corner. I was left to park the car and carry in her bag.

"Slow breaths, Liz. You're doing great!" I encouraged, as the contractions came faster and harder.

Even in labor, my friend was different. Gone was the woman who screamed and cried through her first delivery. Instead, her room was quiet. Liz denied soothing music, ice chips, or a hot shower. Instead, she rocked. Back and forth in the rocking chair next to the bed, she rocked. When a contraction gripped deep inside of her, her only response was to moan and grip the chair's arm rests. She rocked faster and harder until the contraction subsided; then she slowed down to wait for the next one. I sat and watched. Unsure.

"She has Robert's nose," Liz cried softly. "And, look, see that birthmark on her foot? Robert has the same one. She's his. She really is his." Liz uncovered her baby completely and checked her out from head to toe.

"Of course she is," I crooned. "What's her name?"

"Jenny," Liz whispered. "Jennifer Grace."

"It's a beautiful name for a beautiful young lady," Liz's nurse said. "I do have to take her now, though, to be measured and weighed. We have paged her pediatrician and she'll do her newborn exam. Then, we'll draw blood for her lab work. We'll bring her back soon."

I studied Liz's face as she watched the nurse carry her daughter out. Her doctor finished as well and soon we were alone in the room. Endless tears streamed down Liz's cheeks.

"Liz," I said softly. "What did you mean when you said she might not be Robert's?"

"It doesn't matter, now," she replied through the tears. "She is and that is all that matters."

Robert came the next day. He took one look at little Jenny Grace and knew she was his own. After kissing her on the forehead, he hurried out the door to return with a dozen pink roses and four little frilly dresses.

It was Robert who proudly brought Liz and Jenny home from the hospital. He doted on Jenny and Liz settled into mothering again. Amazingly, even Mark adjusted well to the new baby in the house. All seemed to return to normal.

After resting from Jenny's delivery, Liz began to brighten back up. Robert's reaction to Jenny seemed to pull Liz from the prison of pain that she had been locked in for nine long months. It wasn't until years later that Liz shared the details of those dark months and how Jenny was the gift of grace that pulled her out.

chapter 10

"I know we are all responsible for the choices that we make. And, I agree that every choice has a consequence, either good or bad. It may have been Liz's choice that summer night so long ago, but to this day, I still blame Robert," I whisper softly, still sitting at the side of my friend.

"So do I," Dan murmurs. "So do I."

"She never told me," Jenny cries. "She never said anything."

"Of course she didn't," I say, reaching across Liz for Jenny's hand. "Why would she? Robert recognized himself in you. There was no need to say any more. And, when Robert left years later, there was no need to dig up what had been laid to rest."

"I knew about Rob. I always thought he was just a friend," she sniffles.

"He is," I say softly. "Years have erased the hurt. God has

provided the healing. Rob just happened to be there that night long ago when your mom's pain was at its greatest."

"So, he took advantage of a hurting married woman?" Mark accuses.

"No, Mark," I answer carefully. "He never took advantage of your mother. When he drove her home, she was the one to invite him in. She was hurting and she wanted to retaliate. She told me that Rob tried to walk away from her that night so long ago. She was the one who begged him to stay. When he left in the early morning hours, she apologized to him. She promised him he would never see her again."

"Are we really talking about my mom?" he asks. "I can't believe it."

"I know it's hard to believe. It is the reason she wanted me to tell you this story. She knows that we all think the world of her. She wants you to know that she isn't perfect. She never was." I reply.

"Don't forget, Robert hurt her deeply time and time again," Dan replies. "She was deeply wounded and acted out of anger, bitterness, and resentment."

"Which is why she always told me not to be bitter," Mark says thoughtfully, finally understanding his mother's words of wisdom.

"Exactly, Mark," Dan continues. "She didn't just give in to wanting to use Rob for revenge against her husband. She also gave into guilt and bitterness. Which, when mixed with her own regret, sent her into that deep depression. Later, she told me that she got no revenge. Her time with Rob was not worth the dark prison of pain she had to go through."

"Dad had to be furious though," Jenny replies.

"You're assuming he knew," I say with a small smile. "While he did wonder where she was for the second act of the recital, he never knew for sure. He left the recital with another woman and when he got home, Liz had already picked up Mark."

"What would he have done if I hadn't looked like him?" Jenny quietly questions me.

"It doesn't matter," I say lovingly. "Your mom spent nine months fearing his reaction. In the end, it was she who suffered. She often told me, '*if I could do it over, I would have told Robert instead of hiding in shame. If he chose to leave, I would have enjoyed every minute of my pregnancy with Jenny. If he would have stayed and beat me, then I would have had something to worry about.*'"

"Now that sounds like my mom!" Mark smiles. "I'm glad you told us this part of the story too. I needed to know."

"Me too," Jenny sighs, "me too."

"Liz," I lean down and whisper to my friend, "can you hear this? Do you see your kids, Liz? They're amazing. You've done an amazing job with them. And this story, the one you were so ashamed of, it's brought some healing, my friend. Your story is a gift to them. Thanks for letting me tell it."

"Did she ever wear the dresses," Jenny asks quietly, when I finish whispering to Liz.

"No," I reply. "It wasn't until your mom finally told me about Rob that she told me about the dresses. Robert's reaction that night hurt your mother deeper than she ever let on. She had secretly dreamed of becoming a fashion designer after her week with Janet. When Robert destroyed her dress, he also destroyed her dream. She never designed her own gowns again."

"What happened to the dresses that she didn't wear?" Jana whispers.

"Liz is an amazing woman. Even though she was deep into her own prison of pain, she called the music department chairperson. Over the phone, she anonymously donated all of her cocktail dresses, lawn party dresses, and gowns to young women who had nothing to wear for their senior recitals," I quietly answer.

"Mama, you are amazing," Jenny crooned, kissing her again. "I'm so blessed to be yours."

~*~

As Jenny grew, Liz continued to heal. She was made to be a mother. Spending her days with Mark and Jenny fulfilled her. She never did return to the carefree Liz I first met in college, though. Instead, she blossomed into a woman of grace. Everything Liz did, she now did with grace and joy. Including, Robert.

Robert's infatuation with his baby girl was short lived. After a few weeks of playing the role of doting father, he went back to his old ways. He was changed though. He no longer tried to hide his escapades. Blatantly, he defied the university policy of faculty/student relationships. Though many complaints were filed against him, Liz no longer complained. She simply bought a set of bunk beds for Mark. While he slept on the top bunk, she slept on the bottom. The one time Robert dared criticize their new living arrangement, she opened the door and offered him an out.

"Why don't you just kick him out?" I asked one day.

"My children deserve two parents," she said. "And, I promised until death do us part."

"Why doesn't he just leave then?" I huffed.

"Robert needs my money," Liz calmly replied. "If he leaves, he has to live on a professor's salary. Right now, his salary finances his trysts and we live on my trust income. I won't cut him off because I don't want my children to be a statistic. If our marriage fails, it will be Robert's choice.

"You are a better woman than I am," I answered. "I would either throw his stuff on the lawn and change the locks or I would cut off a vital organ while he sleeps."

"Don't think that I haven't thought of either option," Liz laughed, while nursing Jenny. Jenny was an almost perfect baby. With Luke now running instead of toddling around, I longed for another infant.

"When are you going to have another?" Liz teased.

"If only," I answered. "I need Dan around."

"That's a minor detail," Liz replied. "Leave it up to me!"

It felt good hearing the old Liz take charge, but I knew that the problem wasn't Dan. It was his residency. Residency is hard and there is no way around it. I already felt blessed that Dan was chosen to be a resident at the university hospital. When it came time to apply for his residency, I had feared it would take us away from Liz. I was so thankful that he was accepted at the university, I didn't dare complain about his hours. My freelance jobs were plentiful and Luke kept me busy. Instead of pining for a new baby, I loved on Jenny Grace every chance I got.

Dan's next night off was Thursday and my old friend, Liz, was back. She whisked into our apartment laden with gifts. Before I knew it, Liz had dinner in the oven, candles lit, and the music of a new CD filling the apartment. She packed Luke an overnight bag and scooped him up.

"If I remember correctly, you once kept Mark overnight for me. I'm just returning the favor," she laughed. "Besides, Jenny needs a playmate."

I'd be remiss if I didn't say that I needed that night with Dan more than Jenny needed a playmate. After months of quick kisses on his way out the door and notes left on the table, uninterrupted time together was a little slice of heaven. I'd also be lying if I said I didn't enjoy every minute of it. Another gift from my friend.

Liz wasn't disappointed. A few weeks later it seemed as if Jenny would have her playmate. Liz was overjoyed. Dan was ecstatic. I was ill.

"This is good!" Liz exclaimed over the phone line one day. "Remember how sick I was with Jenny? This must be a girl. I'm so glad you are so sick!"

"Shut up, Liz," I mumbled. "You can be excited later. Right now, though, will you please curb your enthusiasm?"

"Ohhh...," Liz giggled. "If I recall, I was extremely grumpy too. It's a girl! It's a girl!" And, with that announcement, she hung up the phone.

However, life isn't fair and enthusiasm promises nothing. When the phone rang right back, I thought it was Liz needing to say "It's a girl!" one more time. If only it were that.

"Liz," I answered.

"No honey, it's Mom," I heard the catch in her voice.

"Mom," I questioned, "is everything okay?"

The silence on the other end of the line was not reassuring. In the few seconds it took Mom to find her voice, a million thoughts went through my head. And, before she said anything else, I knew.

"No," she paused, "no, it's not okay, It's your dad. He's gone. Your daddy's gone, honey."

I don't remember the rest of that conversation. I don't remember hanging up with Mom. I don't remember sliding down the wall and falling into a heap on the floor. And, I certainly don't remember how Liz got there. I only remember the sensation of Luke patting my arm and wondering why Liz was making lunch in my kitchen. She said I called her screaming.

Liz came as soon as I called. She called Mom back and got the details. My father passed away from a major heart attack. Colonel Murph was the strong one, the intimidating one. He was in great shape and usually ran a mile or two a day. However, on that day, he sat at his desk and simply slumped over. His heart stopped beating.

Because of his intense schedule, Dan could not travel with me. Though I missed Dan immensely, I had Liz. It was Liz who sat next to me for the flight out. It was Liz who stood with me as the service men and women filed past to give their condolences to Mom and me. And, it was Liz who held my hand as they lowered my father's casket into the deep, dark hole. Though the pain seemed unbearable, I somehow made it through that week. Sometimes I wonder if Liz carried me through. When that very long week was finished, it was Liz who coordinated the flight home, picked up Mark and Luke from Ash and Bea, and drove us home. She also called my mom to let her know we made it back safely.

Returning home, I felt numb. My days were wrapped in a fog of grief. My head knew my dad was gone. My heart, though, still believed he was invincible. As an only child, I struggled to make sense of it all. Who would take care of my mom now? The United States Army didn't want her. With another baby on the way, Dan and I were maxing out the room in the attic apartment. Where would she go? What should I do? We had a mountain of school debt facing us. What was my responsibility?

If she ever got tired of those questions, Liz never let on. I asked them a thousand times a day and a thousand times she would say, "It's okay. It will be okay." Slowly her words began to sink into my heart and the fog began to lift. Rather than focus on the dead, I began to notice the living again. I saw my son laughing and playing. Instead of looking over him, I looked at him. Instead of ignoring him, I hugged him. And, instead of blocking him out, I heard him laugh. I began to live again.

Loving me through Dad's death seemed to be what helped Liz heal the most. In the midst of my pain, she found purpose. Not only did she stand by my side while I grieved, she also stood with my mom. Liz spent hours talking with Mom on the phone that week, while I rested. She also spent hours calling her parents. In the end, Liz convinced Mom to move to the Ashley Estate and live in the Ashley's guest house. In exchange for her rent, Mom took over the gardening for Bea, who hated dirt and the bookkeeping for Ash, who hated numbers. All three were thrilled with the arrangement.

Life is joy and life is pain. For whatever reason, they coexist on this sphere that spins around the sun. Eight weeks later, I no longer could feel the little life inside me flitter and flutter. Liz and Dan surrounded me as an ultrasound showed our baby's heart was no longer beating. They held my hands and we all cried. I held on to them tightly and my heart constricted. I could not imagine being with anyone else. These two, the ones I loved the most, held my heart.

Standing in the wind and the rain at the Ashley Estate, the three of us laid a small box in the ground. Inside, we had placed the body of our tiny daughter, Joy Elizabeth. On top of her box, we planted a small cherry tree given in memory by Ash and Bea. Ash, Bea, Mom, Luke, and Mark stood with us. It was enough.

Though he was not old enough to truly comprehend, Luke held my hand tightly.

"Mommy, will Jesus let our next baby live?" he asked quietly.

"I hope so, sweetie, I really hope so," I responded. Through my tears I wondered where he ever heard about Jesus.

"I think Papa is holding Baby Joy," he whispered. "Do you

think Papa will tell her that I love her?"

"Yes," I cried. "Papa is loving on her for us. I'm sure he will tell her that we love her."

Later that night, Dan held me close. I felt his steady heart beat. I wondered for the first time how I would ever breathe without him or without Liz. Somehow over the years, my heart had become so intertwined with theirs that I wasn't sure where my heartbeat stopped and their heartbeats started.

"What would I ever do without you or Liz?" I asked, through my tears.

His only answer was to pull me closer. I fell asleep to the beat of his heart.

chapter 11

"It's funny," Luke says, referring to his sister, "I never knew her. Yet, after all these years, I still miss her."

"Because you loved her," I whisper. "Love stamped her into our hearts forever. Though I carried her for only a short time, my heart has never forgotten her."

"Though we never met her face to face, she changed us," Dan remembers. "I think Joy's purpose was fulfilled in those weeks she developed hidden deep inside of Mom."

"What purpose was that, Uncle Dan?" Jenny asks.

"Joy led us to Jesus," he replies. "Actually, the grief we felt was too big and overwhelming to carry alone. And, in our deepest need, we found Jesus."

"I only vaguely remember Papa," Luke continues. "He seemed so big and strong."

"He was," I say, fondly. "He was big and strong and amazing. Growing up with him around was always an adventure. One time he talked me into a bike camping trip. Mom didn't want to bike. She was willing to drive our tent and gear, instead. I should have known better than to think that it would be easy, but Dad always made everything fun. After biking twenty-two miles, we finally got to the campsite. I think I probably cried the last twelve miles. Dad never yelled at me to keep going, he just encouraged me."

"Did you ride home the next day?" Jenny asks.

"Nope, he let me choose," I smile at the memory.

So many memories. So many gifts.

"Luke, I think your Papa is so proud of you," I say looking at my son, now a man. "You remind me of him in so many ways. We could not have named you any better."

"I often talked to Papa when I was in Afghanistan. When I couldn't figure out how to pray, I would look up to the stars on the cold desert nights and tell him about my day. I figured he'd understand," Luke replies softly. "Sometimes I would ask him how to handle a certain problem or how to handle the death all around. Though he couldn't respond, it was usually in the asking that I figured the answer out for myself. I guess God was hearing my prayers after all."

We all ponder Luke's response. We've settled into comfortable silence again. It's late. We're all tired. I look at my friend and watch her heart beat. Slowly and carefully, I lay down next to her putting my hand on her chest. I feel the waning vibration and wonder how many more times her heart beat will reverberate. Even covered up, her body is cold next to mine. I hope my body heat will help warm her. Resting next to her, I close my eyes.

~*~

The weeks and months after laying both Dad and Joy to rest were hard on me. My memory is only of a swirly black darkness. Apparently, I managed to get through each day with some semblance of order, but without any real purpose. Though I knew he was concerned for me and for us, Dan was finishing his last weeks of residency and making up the time that we were at the Estate burying Joy. Liz came often bringing Mark and Jenny to entertain Luke. I stayed in the apartment. I couldn't find the energy to go anywhere or do anything. Buying groceries once a week was my limit. Anything more than that didn't get done. Liz sat by patiently, until she had enough.

"Kris!" she exclaimed one day when I opened the door to her. "It's time!"

"Time?" I wondered.

"You've been in pajamas for days on end. It's a beautiful day. I've got a picnic packed. Let's take the kids to the park.

"Now?" I asked hesitantly. I wasn't ready to live yet. I wanted to stay in this protective cocoon that I had created. This place where I was alive, but barely living. It seemed to be as close to Dad and Joy that I could be and still be with Dan, Luke, Liz, Mark, and Jenny. Though not ideal, I was comfortable in my created space.

"Yes," she said, gently but firmly. "It's time."

She sent me to the shower and somehow found clean clothes for both Luke and me. She promised to take us to the laundromat after the park. She sent Luke and Mark on a treasure hunt to find the missing left shoe to Luke's pair of sneakers and she found the bottom of my kitchen sink. When I emerged with dripping hair, she sent me back to the bathroom to dry it, while she washed my dishes. By the time I was dried, dressed, and presentable, my apartment was too.

Liz had walked over, pulling her kids in a wagon. Luke climbed in with them and held the picnic basket. The day was warm and bright. Luke could hardly contain his excitement at the prospect of fun in the sun. He was like a sponge, soaking it all up. I felt the sun begin to warm my cold heart. Hours later, Liz brought us home, tired and happy. Liz's actions breathed life into me. The warmth of the day, the sound of Luke's laughter, and the sunshine on my nosed helped too.

"How are you?" she asked hesitantly the next day.

"I'm good," I said into the phone. "Really, I'm good. I feel lighter somehow."

"Living. It's good for you," she quipped. I heard the smile in her voice.

"Yes, it is," I answered. "What's on the agenda today?"

"Who says I have an agenda?" she asked, laughing.

"Liz," I laughed back, "you always have an agenda!"

"Well, Miss Know-It-All," she answered, suddenly more serious, "I do have something I've been waiting to talk to you about. Would Luke mind another play date at the park?"

"He'd love it! What time?" I asked, wondering what it was that was so important.

"How about as soon as we all can get to the park?" she replied, hanging up the phone.

When Luke and I arrived forty-five minutes later, Liz was sitting at a picnic table holding a sleeping Jenny.

"She fell asleep in Mark's lap in the wagon," she whispered. "Do you mind sitting here while the boys play?"

Luke joined Mark in the sandbox. The two boys soon had roads built, driving plastic dump trucks and diggers all around their make believe construction site. The only sounds they made were truck noises. Liz and I watched them play in our own comfortable silence.

"Kris," Liz asked quietly, breaking the silence. "Can I talk to you about something?"

"Of course," I murmured.

Watching the boys play, I was amazed. They said little to each other. Yet, they knew exactly what the other was thinking. There was no arguing as they drove over their little hills and dumped their loads. Somehow, these two boys had developed a friendship that mirrored ours.

"I've been hesitant to tell you this because I don't know how it will affect our friendship," she continued, still speaking quietly.

"Huh?" I looked at her, giving her my complete attention.

"Kris, I've found Jesus." Liz announced.

"Was he lost?" I asked, confused.

"No," she continued, "I was."

"Huh?" I asked again. "What are you talking about?"

Memories of growing up in various churches began to flood my mind. Each time the Army moved us, we started over in another church. Mostly, I refused to go to any of the children's programs. Instead, I chose to sit through the long, dry services with my mom. Somewhere along the way, I had heard the stories of Jesus. I remember hearing that He loved children most. I think that story is what made me think I didn't need Him. I thought I was too old, too good, too self-sufficient for Jesus.

"I thought you'd never ask," she smiled.

While Mark and Luke cut new roads and dug deep holes in the sandbox, Liz told me how she found Jesus on the other side of her deep pain.

"When we came home from the hospital with Jenny," she began her story, "I was thrilled, sad, and mad, all together. I was thrilled that Jenny was obviously Robert's, sad that I had reason to even question her lineage, and mad at God for allowing Robert to carry on. Honestly, this was the first time I had thought of God in years. I'm not sure I had consciously thought of God since the last time I sat in my grandma's kitchen and looked at her open Bible on her table. I think that was right before I met Robert. So, not knowing what else to do with this storm of emotion deep within, I called Nana."

"Luke, keep the sand in the sandbox, please!" I interrupted, watching Luke dumped a pail of sand over the edge. "I'm sorry, Liz."

"No problem!" she said, as we watched the boys. "Mark, why don't you help Luke scoop that sand back up with your digger and dump truck. You boys can move that sand back into the

sandbox." With the boys occupied again, Liz continued with her story.

"Nana invited the kids and I for visit. It was as if I couldn't get to her quick enough. Even though we flew to see her, it seemed to take forever to get there. Once we were there, though, time slowed."

"I vaguely remember that you said you were going," I remembered.

"Yes," she said smiling, "I even invited you to go too."

"Yeah, and I didn't want to leave because Dan had a day off coming up," I recalled, returning her smile.

"It's okay," she continued with her story. She gently passed a sleeping Jenny to me for a while.

"Nana welcomed me with open arms. For three days, she loved on me and spoiled my kids. When the kids napped, she opened her Bible. She told me about a baby born in a smelly stable who grew up to die on a cross for my sins. That baby was Jesus, God in human form, and that Jesus on the cross was God paying the price for my sins. Knowing I was a sinner wasn't hard for me. I had not forgotten that night. I just thought I wasn't as bad as Robert or others. However, Nana showed me in her Bible that the cost for all sin is death. Jesus paid that debt for me. Even if I were the only one, He still would have died for me. Those who

accept that He died for them are given the free gift of eternal life. However, the choice was mine. I could choose to accept this gift and my need for a Savior, or I could hear this story and walk away. When Nana explained all of this to me, something inside of me broke open. I sobbed. Through those tears, I recognized my need for this Savior. Sitting there in Nana's farmhouse kitchen, I prayed for the first time. I told God that I was a sinner, that I recognized
all that he has done for me. I asked Him to be Lord of my life. I was finally at peace. Jesus quieted my inner storm."

I looked at Jenny sleeping peacefully in my arms. It all sounded good, even familiar. I remembered hearing it all before. It was the peace Liz talked about that I longed for most. I loved and trusted Liz. I just wasn't sure what to make of her story. It seemed too simple, and too far fetched.

"I recognized this peace in you," I whispered. "I wondered where it came from. You changed and I always thought it was Jenny. You became a woman of grace and peace. Why are you finally telling me now?"

"For a long time I didn't know what to do with my new found relationship with Jesus. I was sure you, Dan, and Robert would think I had just found religion. Though I spoke with Nana several times a week, I didn't really talk to anyone else about it. Nana

continued to encourage me to find a church I liked. I tried a few and felt out of place bringing the kids by myself. Some places treated me like a single mom with a scarlet 'A' on my dress. Other churches treated me like an uninvited outsider. Soon, I was turned off by the people in the church. It was safer to stay home and talk with Nana."

Liz stopped and looked at me for a long time. I could see hesitation on her face. I waited silently. Part of me wanted to hear the rest of her tale, the other side of my heart wanted to stop this discussion of a man named Jesus. I understood her feeling of being turned off by the people in the church. That had been my greatest excuse all these years. I sat quietly. It was easier to enjoy the day and the play date than to reconcile the emotions His name conjured in my soul. Had I not been holding a sleeping Jenny, I may have walked away. Maybe I should have, for her next words stirred those emotions into a raging storm.

"It was Joy that caused me to keep looking," she whispered. "I saw your pain and I felt my own. Dan was at the hospital for long hours and Robert was no where to be found. I needed someone to go to, someone to pray with me, someone to love on me."

"And, I wasn't there..." tears stored deep within me bubbled

over and down my cheeks. "I wasn't there for you."

"Kris, stop!" Liz commanded. "This, right here, is why I have been hesitant to tell you. You are not to blame! God doesn't waste pain. He used my pain to lead me to try one more new church. He directed me to a small building outside of town. A group of incredible people meet there. The first Sunday I walked in, a young girl came and took Mark to children's church as I sat down. As strange as it may sound to you, God met me there. Tears fell as I realized I was home. This church, these people, surrounded me and prayed for healing of this stranger's heart. The people of this church have become my family. They love me and I love them. I would love for you to meet them. I want them to meet you too. Will you come with me this Sunday?"

I hesitated. I had been in a variety of churches in my lifetime. I knew how the church scene worked and I wanted nothing to do with it. A hundred excuses flooded my mind. I wanted to say "NO!" and instead found myself nodding "yes". As I held Jenny, Liz held me and a torrent of tears washed over me. More than anything I wanted peace. If I had to go to church with Liz to find it, then I would go. What I didn't know was that God had a plan for all of us. For the first time in nine weeks, Dan had a Sunday off. Caught in my own hell of grief, I hadn't seen Dan's grief over Joy. Together, we went to church with Liz. These new friends of hers in this little country church loved on us and prayed for us.

Together, we found the peace that Jesus gives.

As Liz said, "God never wastes our pain." He made beauty from our ashes and gave us eternal life.

So many gifts.

chapter 12

I startle awake. I have no idea how long I have been sleeping, or if I truly even slept. Dan reads my mind and understands my struggle.

“You've only been laying with her for about twenty minutes,” he says. “I think you dozed for a little while.”

“I was remembering,” I whisper. “It's good to remember.”

“It is all good,” Dan reminds me. “He never wastes our pain.”

I look around without stirring. Jenny is asleep, leaning on Mike. Luke's eyes are closed and Mark is watching the rain. Jana is quietly knitting. The only sound is the tiny click of her knitting needles as they cross and recross each other, row after row. The silence is full of love and warmth. There are no expectations tonight and no one feels left out. I will look back on this night and remember the golden silence.

Dan reaches over and squeezes my hand. He catches my eye with his, in the light of the lamp. His blue-eyed wink opens the flood gates. It's as if someone has turned a faucet on. All the tears I have been holding in overflow. My heart swells with pain. I had promised myself that I would not sob in front of Liz. I had promised myself that my heart-wrenching weeping would only take place in the shower. I thought I would grieve by myself. He kneels by the bed and gently pulls me to him. I weep into his shirt. Somehow, I know that I will do this again and again and again.

My weeping breaks the golden silence. Jenny wakes and Mark steps out. Luke's cell phone rings and Jana leans in to check on Liz. In the matter of a few seconds, we are all stirring, moving, living.

Isn't this how it is? Even while we wait for death, we live. We, who are alive, keep living. We go on, day after day, saying things like, “I'd die if I had to do that” or “that scares me to death.” We speak so glibly of dying and death. We know nothing of that which we speak.

Tonight, I wonder, is there another way to say that living without Liz scares me to death?

~*~

Church was different. Something I had never experienced

before. It began to feel like home to me, much like my sweet attic apartment. Sunday took on a new meaning to me. No longer the day of the week to avoid church by sleeping in, doing laundry, and going grocery shopping. Instead, it became my favorite day of the week. I looked forward to Sunday with eager anticipation of learning more about this Jesus I had finally found. Dan came when he could and Luke loved Sunday School.

"Mommy, I have something to tell you," he said one Monday morning, while I washed dishes.

"What is it, Sweetie?" I smiled at Luke's serious expression. "It must be serious! Let me dry my hands and we'll talk."

"Mom," he said again, climbing on to my lap. "I want to marry Miss Lindsay." Miss Lindsay was Luke's Sunday School teacher. Apparently, Luke liked Sunday School more than I knew.

"Well, Luke," I stammered, trying hard to swallow the laughter that was about to bubble over. "I think you have to be like 25-years-old or something to get married."

"Oh," he mumbled, clearly dejected.

"Would you like to make her a card instead," I asked.

"YES!" Luke scrambled off my lap and went running for his art box. I finished the dishes and together we opened our art boxes at the table. His was full of construction paper, glue sticks, stickers, markers, and crayons. My art box had my pencils, ink, pastels, erasers, stumps, and colored pencils. While he designed a

beautiful card to take to Miss Lindsay at church, I worked my latest freelance job... the cover of an auto parts manual. Vehicles were not my favorite thing to draw. However, sitting side by side with my son making art together, was way better than any other job I could find.

"Luke," I asked, remembering back to the day we buried Joy. "Who first told you about Jesus? Was it Miss Lindsay?"

"No," he mumbled, working hard. "Papa Murphy told me Jesus loves me every time he hugged me."

Stunned, I watched Luke finish his creation. I had always thought my father kept his religion to himself. He and I never talked about Jesus or my need for a relationship with him. I was surprised that Dad even mentioned it to Luke, and amazed that he did it in a way Luke's young mind could understand. I wished Dad was still around. I wanted to tell him that I had finally found his Jesus. I missed him.

Life settled into a routine. Perhaps it was because Liz and I had both found healing or because sometimes God allows you to rest before the next storm hits. Either way, it felt good.

My vision also changed. I began to notice the small things that brought me peace and joy. Coming out of the dark cloud of grief, I developed a consciousness for things that I had always taken for granted. I noticed the sun shining on dew drops and the sound of the birds chirping in their nest outside the window. When the sun shone down through the clouds or the rain pattered against the roof, I noticed. I never wrote these things down or commented out loud about them, I just noticed them and allowed them to bring joy to my heart.

Dan finished his residency and began the process of finding a job. My perspective had changed some too. I was finally willing to give up the apartment that had been my home for so many years. This place was the very first place my heart ever felt at home. So many incredible memories filled its walls. Though it would hurt me to leave it, I was willing to go with Dan. I was not, however, willing to move far from Liz.

I didn't have to worry, though. Dan had been approached by one of the doctors at Crawford Family Medicine to take a position as a family physician. When he told me, I was ecstatic. Crawford Family Medicine was where Luke's pediatrician practiced. It was a twenty-five minute journey from our apartment to their front desk. Needless to say, Dan accepted the position. Over a business luncheon, he and the partners ironed out the details. I breathed a sigh of relief. A huge gift. Another instance of me worrying about the wrong thing.

"Can I bring Jenny over Thursday morning after I drop Mark off at preschool?" Liz called.

"Sure, you can. I need some Jenny time. What's up?" I asked.

"The Academic Disciplinary Council sent me a letter today. I've been instructed to meet with them Thursday morning at 10 a.m.," she sighed. "It's about Robert."

"Of course it is," I answered. I had lost my respect for Robert years before. "Is he on his way out?"

"I don't know," she said. "The letter simply asks me to appear before them."

"You do know," I continued, "that you do not have to testify against your husband, right?"

"Yes, I know," she answered. "I spoke with Dad's attorney today. He's coming with me. I will answer any question the Council asks me."

"And, I will love on Jenny while you are there. Can I pick up Mark from preschool as well?"

"That would help a lot, and he would love that!" she responded. "I'll even pitch in some money for Happy Meals."

Liz's meeting with the Academic Disciplinary Council did not take long at all. By the time Liz met with them, they had gathered enough evidence to dismiss Dr. Robert Bower immediately... without further pay or references. Liz listened to the charges filed against Robert and the evidence gathered. When asked if she had anything further to add, she simply said, "No comment," and walked out the door. Robert's professional career ended that day.

Liz failed to tell me that she also had a doctor's appointment that day. Soon after she left the campus meeting, she met with her ob/gyn to discuss her latest mammogram. A lump was found, and the doctor wanted an ultrasound done immediately. It was a long day of meetings, waiting, tests, appointments, and more waiting. When she finally finished late in the afternoon, she quietly walked into the apartment.

"That was a long meeting," I exclaimed. "Did they grill you about every single one of Robert's women?"

"No," she said, quietly. She sat down on my rocking chair and stared at the floor. She didn't see Mark and Luke playing with the train set, nor did she see Jenny holding a baby doll upside down. She sat and rocked.

"Liz," I questioned. "What happened with Robert?"

"Robert?" she hesitated. "Oh, Robert was dismissed immediately. They didn't need me. They had already gathered their evidence and made their decision before I arrived. They informed me first simply out of courtesy. Robert found out this afternoon."

"Then what is it?" I whispered, turning from the sink of dirty dishes.

"A lump," she murmured. "Cancer. Stage 2A."

chapter 13

"How much longer does she have, do you think?" I ask quietly, not moving away from Liz.

"It's hard to know. Do you mind moving for a minute?" He asks, offering me his hand. He helps to lift me up so that I don't bump Liz. When I am out of the way, he cautiously sits down next to her and places his hand on her chest.

He's seen death more than I have. This is the first time I have sat and watched death sneak in. Dan, though, lost count years ago.

While he sits and takes her pulse, I gaze at the living amongst us. Mike has taken Jenny to Liz's spare bedroom to nap quietly. I quietly thank the Lord for Mike. Liz and I prayed Mike into this family. Jenny first noticed him when he came to the salon for a routine haircut. More like me than her own mother, she waited quietly until Mike noticed her. Finally, Mike saw the gem that

Jenny is. They've dated now for four years and the wedding is scheduled for May. When Mike proposed during the Fourth of July fireworks, we all thought Liz would be around for a May wedding. We didn't know. Do you ever really know?

"Her heart rate is slowing," he says quietly. "It's also weakening. Lizzie has always been the strong one, though. She could go on like this for a while yet."

His hand stays on her chest. I know that even if she were awake, Liz would not be bothered by Dan's hand. Though they have always been close friends, it is their shared relationship with Jesus that binds these two together. Their love goes deep. He is her brother and her chest is now simply that... a chest. One marked with deep scars that lost it's femininity long ago. One long scar older and more faded than the other, but both still so very visible. In fact, it was Dan who removed the staples and dressed the infected incision site after her second surgery. He joked with her that she had a clean slate ready for whatever tattoo she desired. "*No one to dress this chest for,*" she laughed.

No, awake or asleep, Liz is not bothered by Dan's closeness. In fact, I hope and pray she is comforted by the feel of his strong hand.

"Can I ask you something, Kris?" Mike whispers, coming back into Liz's room. I love Mike for a lot of reasons. Tonight I love him because he is not afraid of waiting with us.

"Sure," I say gently. "What's up?"

"Well, now that Jenny is asleep, I want to tell you how much she is struggling with Liz's death and that her mom won't make it to our wedding," he says slowly and gently. Slow and gentle is how Mike is. He is not a man of many words. He chooses his words carefully. "Not that she isn't grateful that you are willing to walk her down the aisle, but she just really wants to be married with her mom there."

I nod. I understand. I want Liz there too.

"My question is this," Mike continues. "Do you think Pastor Green would be willing to marry us here? Tomorrow?"

I look at the clock. It's now 11:50 p.m., tomorrow is closer than I had realized. Again, I marvel at time and how it waits for no one.

"Wow, Mike," I say. "How does Jenny feel about this?"

"I don't know," he replies. "I'd like to do this to surprise her as well. I know that Liz really wants Jenny to have a fairy tale wedding much like her own. I also know that Jenny promised her mom that she would get married at the Estate with or without Liz. But, will Liz care? I'm not trying to be disrespectful. If Liz has gone on to heaven, does it really matter? I don't care if we still have a formal wedding then. I don't even care if we don't live together until then. I just want to do this for Jenny, now."

"Mike, you are amazing," I say, standing to hug the newest

member of our joint family. "Thank you for seeing Jenny's need and understanding her heart."

This man standing before me is one who comprehends life and death. This is his work... his life calling. He is prepared to see death every time he puts on his uniform. Perhaps it is his work that makes him so wise at a such a young age. Mike knows that life is for the living, and that you live for the living, not for the dead. I have much to learn from this young man. He who is another gift... an incredible gift at that.

"Jon is usually up late," Dan replies gently getting up from Liz's bed. "I'll see if he is available."

~*~

I stand and stare at her, dishwater suds dripping from my hands to the floor. When her eyes reach mine, I know there is nothing left to say. She has spoken the truth. An unseen enemy has invaded her body without consent. This woman who has fought for her marriage is now fighting for her life. Not impressed with how her marriage has gone, I worry about this fight.

"What did the doctor say?" I asked.

"He had an opening next week. Surgery is scheduled for Tuesday," she said.

"Opening?" I ask in disbelief. My emotions surge. How dare

this doctor schedule her like one would schedule a golf outing. I feel rage well deep inside. "What doctor?"

"Dr. Newhart, the newest oncologist at the hospital. He's who my ob/gyn sent me to after the ultrasound today. In fact, Newhart's office did a second ultrasound."

"Newhart? Never heard of him. Makes me think of the old TV show," I grumbled.

"I want to ask Dan about him," I heard her say.

I sloshed my hands back into the sink not sure how to process my emotions. In my typical fashion, I chose to ignore the news, ignore the bearer of the bad news, and immerse myself in something else. I had never done dishes with such gusto.

"Kris," she said, walking into the kitchen. "I like Dr. Newhart."

"Like him?" I hissed. "How can you like someone who tells you that you have cancer?"

"I like him because he gave me hope," she whispered.

"Hope?" I choked out the word.

Liz said nothing else. Instead, she gathered Jenny and Mark, kissed Luke on the head, and walked out the door. The anger that welled inside spilled over into bitter tears. I was mad at God for allowing this disease, mad at the doctor for diagnosing it, and mad at myself for being so self-absorbed that I didn't even reach out to my friend.

When he came home from work, Dan found Luke in front of the TV watching Sesame Street and eating Cheerios right out of the box. He discovered me in our bed hiding under the covers. Though I heard him come in, I pretended to be asleep. He walked out and the bedroom door clicked behind him.

"Mommy's sad," I heard Luke tell him. "So, I'm sad too."

"How 'bout you and I go get a pizza," Dan asked. "Maybe that will help."

"Yes!" Mark yelled. I heard him scramble for his shoes. Apparently, Dan made a game out of getting ready to go because there certainly was a lot of giggling and laughing. Without a word to me, the apartment door banged shut. I was alone and mad at myself for pretending to be asleep.

I emerged from my blanketed cocoon and showered. In this moment, I needed Dan and Liz. I called her and apologized. True to her nature, she told me there was nothing to apologize for. Instead, we made plans to go out for breakfast in the morning with Dan and the kids. I told her I couldn't wait.

When Dan and Luke returned with a mostly empty pizza box, I told them of the breakfast plans. Luke splashed in the tub while Dan and I talked. I told him about Robert's dismissal by the Academic Disciplinary Council. However, I waited until Luke was asleep to tell Dan about Liz's diagnosis. Still angry at God, I could hardly choke the words out.

"Sounds like a horrible, rotten, no-good, very bad day," Dan mused, quoting one of Luke's favorite books. "Only Liz's day sounds a little worse than the day that Alexander, the boy in the book, had."

"Please don't joke," I begged.

"I'm not joking," he said.

He called Liz and she relayed the entire day to him. She told him the details of her various medical appointments. He assured her that she was in good hands with Dr. Newhart.

"Ask her if she's called her parents," I whispered, as he talked with Liz.

Liz assured him that she had called Ash and Bea. They were flying in on Sunday afternoon to stay with the children while Liz was in the hospital. Liz had not been able to reach Robert to tell him the news. No one knew where Robert was or what his plans for Tuesday were. Furthermore, none of us really cared.

Monday evening, Robert finally came home. Ash Ashley wasted no time telling Dr. Robert Bower just exactly what he thought of him. Though I didn't hear the conversation, legend has it that terms such as "spineless creature" and "spoiled child" were used. I've also heard that there were some unmentionable descriptions as well.

While Bea bathed the children and put them to bed, Liz told Robert her diagnosis. She explained that she would be having a single mastectomy in the morning. With his usual flair for dramatics, Robert promptly informed her that he could never love a breast-less woman. With that, he cursed her father and walked out the door. He took none of his possessions with him. Instead, he left everything of value behind.

Bea graciously kept Luke on Tuesday morning while I took Liz to the hospital. Dan had cleared his afternoon schedule and joined us as soon as he could. While Bea was occupied with the children, Ash cleared out all of Robert's clothes and personal belongings. Without a word to anyone, he loaded Liz's car and drove all of Robert's things to the Salvation Army store. When the volunteer asked him if he'd like a receipt, Ash smiled and said, "No thank you. I am hoping something good will come out of these."

In her typical sense, Liz approached her surgery with humor. When the registration clerk asked her why she was there, her response was, "My husband left me and my children no longer nurse. So, I've decided to donate a breast to research. I haven't had much luck with it, anyway."

On a day that might have been a day of sorrow, Liz laughed. All who entered her hospital room laughed as well. And, when it came time to be wheeled to surgery, she took my hand and said, "Life is pain. I don't want to waste my life wallowing in it. Laugh with me and together we won't waste the pain." I could only nod and smile.

When she was brought back into her room, she cautiously reached up to touch the bandages wrapped around her. With a twinkle in her sleepy eyes, she said, "I will now be known as 'The One-Breasted Wonder'." And, with that, she fell asleep.

chapter 14

“She's a wonder, alright,” Dan chuckles, walking back into the room. “I had forgotten that she called herself that.”

“She used that title for a long time,” I reply. “It always brought a few laughs.”

“I just talked to Jon. He was still awake. He's on his way over right now,” Dan continues. “Mike, he'd like to talk to you and then to Jenny. If you both want to do this, he will do it whenever you'd like.”

“Thanks, Dan!” Mike smiles. “Please, don't wake Jenny yet. I'd like to talk to Pastor Jon myself before I tell Jenny.”

“Sure thing,” I say, smiling, too. “It's good for her to sleep, anyway.”

I watch Mike walk out of Liz's room to wait for Pastor Jon Green. Life hasn't been easy for Mike. Yet, here is a young man who hasn't wasted his pain. A major car accident took Mike's mother and younger brother when Mike was just eleven. Mike's father, Jim, was left to raise his young son. The two grieved together and when Mike finished high school, he told his father he wanted to make a difference. He became a paramedic/firefighter because he wanted to help others. The word around town is that if you are in an accident, you want Mike to be the one to respond. It is his compassion and caring, born out of pain, that makes him so good at what he does.

"Jenny's a blessed girl," I whisper to Liz.

"And, Mike is a blessed guy," Mark responds. "They're a great match!"

"So glad you convinced me to pray him into our family," I tell Liz, smiling at Mark.

"We're a blessed family to have him," Mark replies, enjoying our conversation around Liz.

"Yes we are," Dan chimes in.

"And, I am blessed to hear such wonderful things said about me behind my back," Mike jibes poking his head back into the room.

"I thought you had left," I say.

"Obviously," he laughs. "And, I am blessed to be part of a family again. An incredible melded family."

Liz and I count family often on our ongoing gratitude list. I look up on the wall over Liz's bed and see the photo taken last summer. All of us laughing and holding handwritten signs. The photographer handed us each a black marker and piece of white paper. "Write one word that describes your family," she said. "Don't show anyone. When I count to three, turn your paper around for all to see."

There we are... all eight of us, plus Mike, holding signs that say things like "fun," "loving," "special." In the center, Liz sits, with a brilliant scarf draped around her smooth head, smiling biggest of all. Her hands hold a sign that says "gifts." This photo, blown up as large as Liz could order, hangs framed over her bed. And, carved into the handcrafted frame are the words, "Family... life's greatest gift."

~*~

"What's all this?" I asked Liz, walking into her apartment to take her to her first chemotherapy appointment.

"All you wanted to know, and more, about chemotherapy," she answered, motioning to all the pamphlets scattered around her.

"Are you ready," I asked, picking up the nearest brochure.

"Is anyone ever ready?" she questioned back. "No, I'm not ready. I don't think I ever will be. Cancer waits for no one,

though. Let's go."

"Ok," I said, getting back up.

"Last one to the car is a rotten egg," I teased.

"After all that chemo gets in me today, I will be a rotten egg," she quipped back.

As soon as Liz was discharged from her surgery, Dan moved Liz, the kids, and me to the Estate. Liz vacated the apartment that held such awful memories for her and hired a moving company to store her belongings. Luke and I packed just what we would need for a ten-month hiatus. We all piled into a rented van and Dan drove us to western New York. Liz slept most of the journey. After making sure we were all settled in with Ash, Bea, and Mom, Dan drove himself back to the lonely little attic apartment. Throughout the duration of Liz's cancer treatment, he would come whenever he could. The rest of the time, he worked extra hours and took every "call" shift he could to offset his loneliness. And, each month, he would pay either a double or a triple payment on his school loans. A hidden gift.

Dan collaborated with Dr. Newhart to schedule Liz's chemo and radiation in Buffalo, so that we could be near Ash, Bea, and my mom. The kids were excited to have Papa, Nana, and Grandma Murphy to dote on them. Our parents were thrilled to be part of their lives. Liz relaxed knowing that Mark and Jenny were taken care and deeply loved. She bought a kindergarten curriculum for 5-year-old Mark and home schooled him on her good days. On her bad days, we all pitched in to be sure that he got his school work done. Soon, almost 3-year-old Jenny, and, 4-year-old Luke wanted to do school with Mark. Before we knew it, we had our own little preschool/kindergarten room set up with three eager students. I had brought my art box and work with me, to work between trips to Buffalo. Dan flew up whenever he could. All in all, it was a fabulous arrangement.

There is no pamphlet, brochure, or flier that can prepare a person for chemotherapy. The greatest exercise of self-discipline is the act of willingly walking into a cancer center, sitting still for the IV, and remaining in the recliner while a lethal pharmaceutical cocktail slowly drips into your vein. I've heard it said that it is hard to be the one receiving the chemo. In my personal experience, it's much harder to be the one watching. Every single time the IV drip began, I wanted to run. Deep within me was the urge to take off for parts unknown and to never look back. Only by the grace of God was I able to sit next to my friend for six hours and watch.

Liz, however, embraced chemo days. She saw these days as her days to reach out to others. She took every opportunity to love on the people around her, patients and staff alike. By the end of her first treatment day, she had endeared herself to all of them. She became their favorite patient and they were all rooting for her. She was loved by all.

It was the day after chemo that was always her worst day. It was the day I hated the most. She would plan ahead and have all kinds of surprises planned for the kids. She did this so that they would be preoccupied while she lay on the bathroom floor so sick she could hardly lift her head. She adamantly prohibited any of us from helping her on that day. According to her rules, we were to leave her alone and enjoy the day for her. I never was one to follow her rules.

Every single time she lay on the bathroom floor, I sat on the edge of the bathtub reading aloud to her from the Psalms of David. Eventually, after there was nothing left and her body mercifully relented, she would crawl to her bed and sleep the rest of the day. I would slip out and find solace sitting under Joy's cherry tree or walking the trails Ash had groomed through his woods. Many prayers were uttered during that time away from the ears of little ones. Later, I would find the kids and assure Mark and Jenny that Mommy was resting well. Regardless of how hard the day had been, Liz always pulled herself out of bed to be the one to read their bedtime story and tuck Mark and Jenny in for the night.

Eventually, we all fell into a good routine. After Liz's chemo day and sick day, she would rally and join us, living life on the Estate. So much of those ten months were gifts we counted later. Nature walks through the woods with the kids, crafts with construction paper and glue sticks, and snowy days with books and hot cocoa made our gratitude list, as did the time with our parents. Bea graciously stepped out of her society roles. Instead, she embraced the mayhem in her home. She hung every colored page and paper craft for all to admire, counted and sorted M&M's with little hands, and read The Very Hungry Caterpillar *at least a million times. Ash wrestled with the boys and gave Jenny countless horsey rides. Mom Murphy taught us the names of trees, the songs of the birds, and the footprints of the forest animals. Countless gifts.*

"No wig!" Liz demanded when her hair began to fall out. "It's too hot and itchy."

"How do you know?" I questioned. "You haven't even tried it."

"Because it looks hot and itchy!" she reasoned. I had long ago learned that arguing with Liz's reasoning did no good.

"Ok," I retorted. "How are you going to keep your head warm?"

"A scarf," she replied. "And, lots of them! Feel like shopping?"

I never felt like shopping. However, if my friend felt good enough to go, who was I to disagree? We spent the day visiting several boutiques, trying many different scarves, and laughing our fool heads off. It has been said that laughter is the best medicine. If that is true, we both got a great big dose of good stuff that day. After buying several beautiful scarves, we found a sweet little bistro that served us soup and sandwiches for lunch. Great food, great conversation, a great time filled our day. It was a day full of the gift of love, laughter, and friendship.

The next day the laughter continued when Liz made me shave the remainder of her hair. Who could resist shaving a mohawk first? The kids got in on the fun when they saw Liz's funny hairdo. By the end of my one day stent as a barber, Liz's head was smooth. Mark sported a mohawk for a few pictures and then a smooth head like his mother's. Jenny and Luke decided they would rather just watch than get too close to my hair clippers. We all laughed and took many pictures of Liz and Mark's matching hair style.

chapter 15

"It wasn't the only time our hairstyles matched," Mark quietly replies.

"I know," I say. "You've always been such a good sport about matching your mom's smooth head."

"It was the one thing I could do," he sighs. "I never knew she was sick with cancer. I never knew that the chemotherapy made her so sick."

"Each time she had chemo," I reply, "she got very ill from the side effects. She never wanted you and Jenny to worry about her."

"It's weird," he muses. "I never worried about Mom. I worried about where my dad was, what he was doing, and if he'd come back to us, but I never worried about Mom."

"Then all of her effort paid off," I say smiling.

"I think my Mom was bigger than life to me," he continues.

"Everything she did, she did amazingly well. In my young mind, I knew that cancer would be no match for Mom."

"She did fight it well," I respond, "until her body just couldn't fight it any longer."

We both sit quietly and watch Liz for a few moments. If only I could bottle up time, I would uncork the time spent at the Estate and live it over and over again.

"You know," Mark continues, as if reading my mind, "those months here at the Estate are really my first memory of this place. I think they are why I have fallen in love with this little slice of heaven and why I keep coming back. Do you remember the spring, nine years ago, when Papa had the pond dug?"

"Yes!" I smile. "What an adventure. You and Luke reverted to little boys when you saw all the earth movers and diggers."

"Oh yeah!" Luke chimes in. "For a 14-year old kid, those were like real life toys. Too bad we dug up the south lawn when the contractor let us drive them. I'm not sure Grandma Murphy ever truly forgave us for the deep ruts in her beautifully manicured yard."

"That pond, though," I remember, "brought many hours of fun entertainment. When Papa saw how much you four enjoyed swimming in it and fishing from its banks, he told us that he wished he would have had a pond dug years before."

"There certainly is something about this home and the land

that surrounds it," Dan joins in. "If I believed in such things, I might say it's magical."

Dan and Mark nod, each of us lost in our own sweet memories of time spent here... this place we call the Estate. Recollections of swimming on hot summer days, camping in the woods with Grandpa Murphy's old Army tent, and bonfires under the stars fill the room. For this moment, we are all lost in the remembering.

"Not magical," I muse, "healing. This home and all that surrounds it is a balm to hurting hearts."

"I wish Mom would find healing here again," Mark says, softly.

"She is, Mark." Dan replies, gently looking into Mark's hurting eyes. "She is finding healing. Soon, she will be in the arms of Jesus and there will be no more pain and no more tears. She will be healed. She will be whole."

Silent tears spill over Mark's eyes. Healing for Liz is what we all desperately desire. We also know that we will be the ones left hurting. Our hearts struggle to reconcile those two opposing ideas.

~*~

Christmas at the Estate was breathtaking. Bea spared no expense in decorating for the holidays. The day after an enormous Thanksgiving feast, we all donned boots, hats, gloves, and scarves.

Ash took us all on a hunt for the perfect Christmas tree. Though the air was crisp, no snow had yet fallen. The natives were getting restless for some of that fluffy white stuff.

"I wish it would snow," Liz said softly, as we all hiked along the brown path scattered with fallen leaves.

"Me too, Mommy!" exclaimed Mark. "Then Luke and I can build a huge snow fort surrounded by a snow city. We'll even make a snow planet!"

"I wish I had your energy," I said, laughing at Mark.

"The snow would be so pretty," remarked Liz. "And, it would cover up all these dead leaves."

Suddenly, I realized why Liz pined for snow. Not yet to the half-way point of her chemo treatments, she had already seen enough of death and dying. Though snow would not solve any one's problems, it could be a great diversion. Liz was feeling a deep need for some beauty to cover the death all around.

"Maybe it will snow soon," I remarked. "I can't even imagine how gorgeous the Estate is in the snow."

A few minutes later, Ash, Mark, and Luke found the "perfect" Christmas tree, a six-foot white spruce. With a lot of effort, the little boys helped Ash chop it down, each getting one turn with the ax. Together the three hefted the tree into the back of Ash's pickup truck that Mom and Bea had driven down the lane. Mark and Luke insisted on riding in the back of the truck with the tree. So, with Jenny sitting on Mom's lap in the cab and Ash and the boys in the back with the tree, Bea drove back to the house. Liz and I followed slowly on foot.

"How would I do this without all of you?" she asked.

"You wouldn't, of course," I replied, casually, enjoying the walk.

When Liz didn't answer, I looked over at her. Without making a sound, tears streamed down her cheeks.

"What is it?" I asked.

"Hard. It's just hard. I worry about the kids a lot. They have no father to speak of and their mother is fighting cancer. It just doesn't seem fair."

"Well," I said, cautiously. "I don't think your kids are suffering much. They have six adults who love them tremendously and who are building into their lives on a daily basis. I know their little hearts still carry a wound from Robert leaving. However, under the circumstances, you are doing an amazing job."

"Thanks. I hope someday to be well enough, again, to do an amazing job. Right now, you, Dad, Mom, and Grandma Murphy are doing the amazing job. I have been benched to the sideline."

"It's all of us together, my friend, all of us together." Neither Liz nor I were very demonstrative people, but I slung my arm across her shoulder for the walk home. We arrived just in time, too. Papa could hardly unload the tree around the three little

bodies dancing in the way.

December came without snow. It was brown and dreary. Liz's mood seemed to match. She seemed to slip further into herself, though she pretended well for the kids. Often, we would find her in the conservatory playing the piano she first took lessons on, all those years ago. Occasionally, she would play a Christmas carol or two. Mostly, though, she played Chopin's dark and melancholy pieces.

"What do you think is going on inside of her?" Ash asked me one day, while we stood in the doorway listening to Liz play.

"I think she's sick and tired of being sick and tired," I replied. "I also think it's hard to face your own mortality when you have two little ones to care for. Especially when you feel alone."

"But, she's not alone," he murmured. "She has us."

"I know that and you know that," I replied. "Soon, she'll know it, too. Right now, I think she's mourning the loss of her fairy tale dream."

Ash made no comment. We stood and listened for a few more minutes. He turned and squeezed my arm, "Thanks for bringing her here."

"I could think of no better place," I said, squeezing his hand in return.

With that, he turned and walked to his office down the hall. Bea had shared the story of the placement of Ash's office with

Mom and me just yesterday. Once Liz began piano lessons, Ash moved his office down from the second floor. He took over what was originally the library for his business transactions, so that he could be near Liz while she played. Nothing moved Ash as much as Liz's music.

Though there was no snow, the Estate was filled with holiday activities all throughout the month of December. All three children were right in the thick of things. Mark and Luke helped Bea decorate the front porch, the stairwell, and, of course, the Christmas tree. Jenny helped Mom in the kitchen making cookies, candies and cakes. In the schoolroom, the kids worked diligently on homemade cards to go with the sweets. Liz had specifically asked us to deliver our goodies to the oncology ward at the hospital. When all the cards were made and the sweets were boxed up, Liz's counts were low. So, we went without her and missed her the entire time we passed out the treats.

Several mysterious deliveries were made to the house during the week before Christmas. Many boxes brought curious glances. None, so much, as the enormous box delivered on December 22. Two delivery men brought it to the door. When Ash saw them, he took over overseeing the delivery. I saw him slip them a tip as he asked them to carry the mysterious package to the guest house. When he realized that he had been seen, he put his finger to his lips and winked. I could hardly wait to see the mystery. I had already guessed who it was for.

Dan arrived on December 23. Almost immediately, he and Ash hurried away to the guest house and the mysterious package. Ash was not the only one being secretive. It seemed as if everyone, including the kids, were hiding things and acting peculiar. I laughed out loud when I saw Mark holding his hands behind his back hiding a large construction paper angel bigger than he was.

"Shh, Aunt Kris!" he chided. "It's a surprise. Is Mom around?"

"Ah, no," I giggled. "She's resting."

"Good!" Mark scurried to his room to hide his precious gift.

With three small children in the house, Christmas morning dawned bright and early. Soon we were all awakened with the shouts of "It's Christmas! It's Christmas!!" Luke grabbed my hand and pulled me into the front room to see the gigantic pile of gifts stacked under and around the tree. He joined Mark and Jenny as they danced around. They simply were unable to contain their excitement.

Ash, in a Santa hat, made the children sit down as Mom brought in coffee for the adults. Suddenly she said, "Liz! Look!"

We all looked up to see Mom Murphy looking out the window. Big fat snowflakes were falling and an inch of the fluffy stuff covered the ground. An awe-inspired quiet fell over all of us as we watched the snow drop silently to the ground. The hush lasted for about a minute before the kids remembered the gifts. One by one Papa passed out presents from under the tree. Sitting with her feet tucked under her and a mug of hot coffee in her hands, Liz smiled for the first time in weeks. It was the most beautiful sight that morning and the best gift any of us could have received.

Eventually Ash handed Liz an envelope. She opened it, read the letter inside, and gave him a quizzical look. Without a word to any of us, she disappeared. Ash winked at me and started to follow Liz. We all followed him.

"We used to do this when she was younger," he said to Dan and me.

"Do what?" I asked.

"A scavenger hunt," he winked at Dan.

"Wait a minute," I whispered. "Does this have anything to do with the guest house?"

Though neither answered me, they both smiled. Soon, I heard the back door open and close. Before we could get boots and coats on the kids, Liz came back with a huge smile and tears in her eyes. She wrapped her arms around Ash's neck and said, "Thank you! Thank you! Thank you!"

"Come on, Dan," he said, unwrapping himself from Liz's embrace. "Let's move it over here and we will all enjoy it." The two of them stomped through the snow to the guest house and brought back Liz's Christmas gift... a beautiful concert harp. As

the snow continued to fall, Liz tuned her new instrument and spent the rest of the day playing Christmas carols beautifully.

Eighteen inches of snow fell that day and a new tradition was born. Every Christmas since then, we have had at least one scavenger hunt in honor of Papa. None, though, have brought as much joy as that harp. We were all given day full of Christmas gifts, seen and unseen.

chapter 16

"Remember the Christmas when Dad finished the room above the garage and sent all four of us on separate scavenger hunts to find it?" Luke remembers.

"The F.R.O.G. It was his Christmas gift to all of you kids that year," I recall smiling. "If my memory serves me correctly, Mark had the hardest scavenger hunt and Ryan had the easiest. In the end, you all ended up there about the same time. My favorite part of that day was when you and Mark named it the F.R.O.G., Finished Room Over Garage."

"Not the most creative name, but definitely the best gift ever!" Luke exclaims. "All the kids in the neighborhood hung out because of the old pinball machine and the ping-pong table."

"I think they hung out there because Aunt Liz kept the little refrigerator in it stocked with juice and sodas," I laugh. "The only regret I have about that room is that I didn't insist that your father install a bathroom up there. There was always a line of kids in and out of the kitchen to use the bathroom in the house."

"It took a lot of time to do that room. Especially considering that I didn't want to spend a lot of money to hire it done. I wasn't sure I would get it finished in time. In the end, your mom and Liz put in a lot of hours with me. Seeing the looks on your faces when you completed the scavenger hunt and ended up in the room was worth all the long hours," Dan reflects. "It was important to me that we knew who your friends were and what you were doing with them. The easiest way to accomplish that was to build you a room in our house where you could hang out and still be safe."

"That was Papa's last Christmas with us," Mark quietly remarks. "I think he enjoyed watching us running like banshees through the house and yard finding the clues. I remember how he laughed and slowly followed along."

"Your Papa was always bigger than life to me," I respond. "When Nana Bea died eight years ago, Ash really slowed down. I never really thought about their marriage until after she was gone. I think they had a much better marriage than anyone ever knew. His heart was broken when she was gone. I think his heart attack, seventeen months later, was his heart refusing to live any longer without her."

"Not sure that would be the medical explanation," Dan quips.

"But, he sure did love that woman!"

"I marvel that he adopted Ryan and me like we were his own," Luke states. "It wasn't until I was twelve that I fully understood that he wasn't really my Papa."

"He and Bea had more than enough love to share with all of us," I answer. "All of our lives are richer for the love they invested in us."

Liz stirs again. Dan and I adjust her pillows. She seems to be restless. She refuses a sip of water and another pillow adjustment. She says nothing, but it's obvious that she needs something. Finally, she catches Dan's eye.

"Do you want more morphine?" Dan asks, gently.

Jana steps out and soon returns with Liz's next dose. I wonder how many doses they've planned for... how many more times they expect to give her pain medicine. My heart hurts at that thought and I know there is no drug to alleviate my kind of pain.

~*~

"I miss church," Liz casually mentioned one day, on the way to her fourth radiation appointment.

"Me too," I said.

"I'm ready to go back," she replied.

"Go back to the campus area?" I questioned.

"No, I have nothing there but bad memories," she answered. "I want to go back to life, to church, to friends and acquaintances that are still there. I'm ready to move on."

"Then let's go!" I exclaimed. The months away from Dan were taking their toll on me. As much as I loved Liz, and as much as I was grateful for the time with Ash, Bea, and Mom, I was ready to be a family of three again.

Liz spent her next few weeks of radiation contacting real estate agents. After settling on one agent in particular, Liz gave her list of "must haves." Her list was long. It included things like a garage, a finished basement, and a gas log fireplace. It must be in an upscale subdivision and a good school district. The house Liz sought must not have paneling on any of its walls or a chain-linked fence. I was never sure if the list helped or hindered the agent, but Liz spoke with authority. After her initial credit check, the agent was more than willing to bend over backward for Mrs. Bower. I would chuckle every time I would hear the phone conversations. I could only imagine the voice on the other end saying, "Yes, Mrs. Bower. Of course, Mrs. Bower. Whatever you would like, Mrs. Bower."

Apparently, Liz was also on the phone when I wasn't around. Our wedding was not the only surprise she and Dan cooked up. While Liz's agent was looking for a home for Liz to buy, I had no idea she was also looking for a home for us as well. Apparently the number one item on Liz's list of considerations was that there were two houses for sale in the same subdivision. Also unknown to me, Dan was her liaison. He walked through many houses with the realtor. Dan's "yes" or "no" was also Liz's "yes" or "no." She trusted him implicitly.

Dan called Liz and told her he found her a home. After thirty minutes of describing the layout, the color scheme, and the amenities, she was sold. She called the realtor and faxed in a written offer. Within a week, the paperwork was underway for Liz to own her first home.

"Is there another house for you guys?" she asked Dan.

"There aren't currently any for sale. The realtor assures me, though, that there will be one soon. Let's get you settled. Kris and I will come later."

His answer satisfied Liz and she met with Ash's attorney. In the attorney's office, she closed on her new house. She was a first time home owner.

Ten months, one week, and two days after we all moved to the Estate, we moved back home. Liz's last blood work showed her to be in remission. We were elated. Even though we thoroughly loved the time at the Estate, we missed our church family tremendously. They prayed Liz through these rough months of chemo and radiation. We were ready to go back and report the wonderful answer to prayer.

After many tears, hugs, and waves goodbye, we all piled into another rented van and Dan drove us home. The trip went fast, as we all told Dan stories of our time at the Estate. Even Jenny got in the action by telling "Unca Dan" about the squirrels and the chipmunks that came to feast in the bird feeders. I reached out and held Dan's hand most of the way home. This man who promised himself to me "for better or for worse" just willingly gave me up for ten months. Though the nights in the attic apartment were lonely, he never complained. He simply loved on me from afar. Gifts. Too many to count.

When we pulled into town late that night, Dan did not drive to the apartment. In fact, he drove past our exit off of the freeway. I looked at him sleepily. He simply smiled. Keeping secrets was Dan's specialty and there was no getting him to give it away.

"Let's wait until morning. I'd like the kids to see it in the daylight," Liz spoke up from the back seat.

"Sorry. Can't do that," was Dan's only reply.

Ash was the only one I had ever seen pull off a surprise for Liz. I was about to see another accomplish that great feat. Liz had no idea what Dan was up to. I sat and reveled in the glory of another surprise.

Fifteen minutes later, Dan pulled into the entrance of one of the area's newest subdivisions. Lamplight lined the quiet streets. The modest houses all had large yards, most with a swing set or play house. Signs of children.

Finally, Dan turned into a quiet cul-de-sac and parked the car on the street. Two identical dark houses stood facing each other. One house slightly smaller than the other still had the "For Sale" sign in the yard.

"Dan, it's beautiful," Liz whispered, looking at the house with the "For Sale" sign.

"Yes, it is," he smiled at her. "But you are looking at the wrong house. Your house is the bigger one." He handed her a key ring.

"Go," he said. "Both of you, go. I'll stay in here with the kids for a few minutes. They're still sleeping, it's okay."

As quietly as two giggling women could go, Liz and I sneaked out of the van and ran up the dark sidewalk. As she turned the key and opened the door, I found a light switch.

"Oh, my," was all Liz could say.

Dan had done it. He had completely surprised Liz. He hired the same moving company that moved Liz's belongings into storage to move those same things to this new house. He also hired the wife of an associate, an interior decorator, to oversee the placement of Liz's furniture. She did a marvelous job of unpacking and setting up Liz's new home. Liz was speechless.

We wandered from room to room gazing at Liz's new home. Occasionally, Liz commented about her closet or the window seat in the living room. Mostly, though, we explored silently, taking it all in. I moved about amazed at Dan's ability to choose a home that so completely reflected Liz. She moved about touching surfaces and opening closed doors. This new house, this home, was a new beginning for her. It could not have been a better one.

"Kris," Liz called from the kitchen. "There is something in here for you."

"Coming," I answered. I couldn't imagine what could be in the kitchen for me.

"Here," she handed me an envelope with my name written in Dan's barely legible scrawl.

Dear Kris, I know you needed to be with Liz and that you two need each other. I need you both, too. These last ten months have been torture being here without you. I know our little attic apartment is home to you and you love it much. I hope you love being with Liz and me more than that apartment though. I put an offer on the house across the cul-de-sac. The offer is contingent on you saying "yes" to it. If you like it, we can all be together again. All my love, Dan

Standing in the kitchen with tears streaming down my face, I fell in love all over again. I handed the note to Liz. We both screamed, jumped up and down, and danced around Liz's new kitchen. In all of our commotion, we didn't hear Dan and the kids.

"What is it Mommy?" Mark asked, sleepily.

"Oh, sweetie," Liz scooped him up. "This is our new home. Uncle Dan picked it out for us. Isn't it wonderful?" She looked at Dan through tears in her eyes and said, "The best part, Mark, is that Uncle Dan, Aunt Kris, and Luke will be our neighbors."

"Yippee!" Mark yelled, looking at all of us. Then, in a quiet voice he said, "Can I go to bed now?"

"Yes, Mark," I kissed him. "You have a brand new bedroom to sleep in and tomorrow Uncle Dan, Luke, and I will be back to visit you."

Dan handed Jenny to Liz and picked Luke up. The three of us walked out of Liz's new home and drove back to the attic apartment. While Dan tucked Luke in, I wandered around my favorite place touching every surface, reliving a myriad of memories. In my own way, I was saying goodbye to the very first home I ever had.

Are you mad at me?" Dan whispered, sliding his arms around my waist.

"No," I answered quietly. "Not at all. Little by little life has changed me. I love this little apartment, but it's really only a place to stay. Home is where your loved ones are. I will be home any time I am with you."

Without a word, Dan scooped me up and carried me to our bedroom. One last incredible memory in that first home of mine and an ongoing gift to go with us.

As the sun first came over the horizon, the pitter patter of little feet scurried across that apartment floor. Soon, the three of us snuggled together for a few more hours of sleep. Our little family of three together again.

chapter 17

"Did you ever plan to live so long in that house?" Luke asks Dan.

"No, I can't say that I did," Dan replies. "But I did learn long ago to not make very many plans. God has a way of rearranging most of the plans I ever made."

"After moving so much as a child, I can't believe we lived there as long as we did," I say. "It was a great place for you kids to grow up. We had super good neighbors and the school district was one of the better ones in the state. Looking back, I can't imagine being anywhere else."

"It's kind of funny to think that Ryan has only ever lived in that house and this one," Luke muses.

"I think it is kind of strange to him too," I respond smiling. "When he came yesterday, he helped Liz and me list all of the wonderful things we could remember from those days in the cul-de-sac. Our list was full of thanksgiving for the gifts that living there brought."

"We've been blessed with three homes," Dan says, softly. "Mom's favorite attic apartment, the cul-de-sac house, and this Estate. Though this beautiful home belongs to the Ashley's, somehow over time, it has become our place too."

Luke and Mark nod, each of us lost in our own sweet memories of time spent here, this place we call the Estate. Recollections of picking sweet cherries, swimming on hot summer days, camping in the woods with the old Army tent, and bonfires under the stars fill the room. For this moment, we are all lost in the remembering.

"Thanks Dad," Luke says. "I never realized how blessed I was growing up."

"Most of us don't, Son," he replies. "I have lived much of my life just going through each day without stopping to notice the blessings I overlook. I think learning to stop and notice the gifts has made me a more grateful person. I only regret not learning this sooner."

In the distance, we hear a knock on the back door. Mark jumps up to answer it before he hears Mike say, "I've got it."

Pastor Jon Green steps through the door, into the laundry room, dripping from the cold November rain. Leaving his coat, umbrella, and wet boots there, he follows Mark to the kitchen in his stocking feet. The Ashley Estate stopped following society's protocols long ago. Friends now enter through the laundry room, rather than entering through the imposing front oak doors into the formal foyer.

"Here's a hot cup of coffee," Mike offers. "Unless you'd rather have tea or hot cocoa?"

"Coffee would be fine, Mike," Pastor Jon says, wrapping his cold hands around the steaming mug. "Thanks! The warmth from the fireplace feels so nice tonight."

"If you'd like, we can sit around the table here and enjoy the fire," Mike suggests.

From Liz's room, I can hear the murmurs of their conversation. Apparently, Liz can hear them too. She stirs.

"Good morning, sleepyhead," I say, though it is barely morning.

Liz doesn't say anything as she looks around the room. Her eyes touch the four of us as she keeps looking.

"Jenny?" she rasps.

"She's sleeping in the next room," I answer, gently. "Mike took her in there. She was exhausted."

Liz nods. She's completely aware of how difficult this is for each of us. She's also aware of how much Jenny has been here.

"Jon?" she rasps again.

"Yes, Jon Green is here. He came at Mike's request," I answer.

"Why?" she whispers.

"Because he asked him to, nosey," I say, smiling. "If there is anything else to tell you, I will certainly let you know."

Liz answers me with a look that makes me laugh out loud. In no uncertain terms, she is not pleased with my reply. Liz likes to be the one in control; the one in the know. I laugh at her dilemma. She attempts to give me a dirty look. She has no energy to fight me on this. In a moment, a rush of emotions flood my soul. She sees the storm in my eyes and winks at me, knowing there is nothing left to say. I will so miss her!

~*~

Five weeks after Liz moved into her house, Dan, Luke, and I walked out of the attic apartment. For the last time, we closed the door behind us. Liz, Mark, and Jenny were standing in our new driveway when we drove up with the moving truck behind us. Three hours of confusion and conundrum ensued. In the end, the moving truck was empty and our new house was full of boxes. Dan ordered pizza for all and Liz began her magic. She put me to work unpacking and moving things around until she found just the right home for each and every item I owned. As a box was emptied, it was commandeered by Mark.

Mark and Luke created a city out of the empty moving boxes in the empty bedroom. Apparently, they had a bank, a library, and a school, as well as having a house for each of them. Each new box became a new building in their make-believe town. And, right smack dab in the middle of their town, Jenny fell asleep in the box marked "hospital."

It probably goes without saying that I loved my new house across from Liz's. Much like the attic apartment, it had quaint little features. Luke loved the spaciousness of it. He not only had his own bedroom; he also had a playroom in the basement to set up his train tracks. The fact that Mark could come over any time to play trains with him was the added bonus. Dan loved it because we were all together. He made Liz and me promise to never leave him again.

It didn't take long in our little house for me to discover the one last thing that we brought with us from the little attic apartment. This time I knew before either Liz or Dan. Because I wasn't extremely sick or grumpy, I kept the news to myself for awhile.

Emotions that I thought had long been laid to rest with Joy surfaced again. I feared losing this baby. Yet, in spite of my fears, I found myself getting excited at the prospect of a new little one in our new home. I held on to my secret until after my first doctor's appointment.

"Is Dan available?" I asked Beth, his receptionist, as I walked into the Crawford Family Medicine office.

"Hi Kris! He's in with a patient now and then has a 20 minute break. Do you want to wait out here?" she asked me, after checking his schedule.

"Is there an empty exam room?" I wanted to know. "I'd like to surprise him, if I can."

"Sure!" she said excitedly. "Come on back!"

Lori, Dan's nurse, saw me in the hallway and pointed to Exam Room 3.

"You can hide in here," she said giggling.

"Great! Oh, and can you bring in the fetal doppler?" I asked, winking.

"Ohhhh!" she giggled some more as she went and got the doppler for me.

I took it from her and gently closed the door to Exam Room 3. Lori raised the flag on the outside of the door to signal Dan that he had one more "patient." It didn't take long before there was a quick knock at the door and Dr. McClintock walked in.

"Kris!" he exclaimed. "What are you doing here? Is everything alright?"

I held up the fetal doppler monitor in my hand and said, "I thought you might want to hear your baby's heartbeat."

Later that evening, we all gathered around Liz's dining room table for a celebratory dinner. She pretended to be mad at me for not telling her. She didn't fool me, she had a twinkle in her eye just like the rest of us. After the events of the past couple of years, a new baby was certainly something to celebrate.

Mark started first grade and Luke kindergarten. Liz opted to keep Jenny home for one more year, rather than send her to preschool. We three girls spent many hours shopping for the new baby. When I was expecting Luke, there was no extra money to buy things for the baby. I took whatever hand-me-downs I could find and did without. With this little one, though, I was throughly enjoying the shopping, decorating, and designing. Together, Liz and I designed an antique toy nursery with an old Red Flyer wagon that we unearthed at an obscure antique store.

For the most part, things were uneventful. The boys loved school. Work was going well for Dan and my pregnancy progressed without incident. The only gray cloud on the horizon was the unknown whereabouts of Robert. During our time at the Estate we had an unspoken agreement that any talk of Robert was taboo. However, now that Liz and the kids were settled in, and doing so well, I broached the subject.

"What are you going to do about Robert?" I asked one day.

"Why do I have to do anything?" she retorted.

"Don't you think the kids need closure?" I asked, probing further.

"Do you think my kids are having a hard time adjusting?" Liz asked back. She was a pro at answering a question with a question. "Aren't you the one who assured me they were well-adjusted?"

"Your kids are doing fine," I stammered, "but, don't you want to move on?"

"What?" she asked back, again. "I've survived a mastectomy, chemo, and radiation. I've purchased my own home and I am raising two incredible children. I think I have moved on, don't you?"

"Yes," I hesitated. "You are doing great. Mark is doing great. Jenny is doing great. I just don't want Robert to waltz right back in."

"What makes you think I'll let him back in?" she questioned.

"Would you please stop answering my question with a question?" I sputtered. "You know, I only ask because I care."

"Yes," Liz laughed. "I do know that. I told you before that I will not divorce Robert. Besides, I really don't know where he is and I don't want to get into the stress and expense of trying to find him just to divorce him."

With that answer, the question was dropped. Liz continued to answer to "Mrs. Bower" and she continued to wear her wedding ring. To all those observing her, she was a married woman. She never looked at another man, nor did she do anything to encourage another man. Not that there weren't opportunities. Liz kept her hair short after the chemo and the "One-Breasted Wonder" was as stunning as ever.

Though my pregnancy was uneventful, apparently the delivery wouldn't be. Breech is how this child wanted to come and every effort to turn him failed. In the end, he came via C-section. Early in the morning, as Liz and Jenny walked Luke and Mark to the bus stop, Ryan Daniel McClintock made his entrance into this world. After his birth, I had complications. I hemorrhaged for several hours. Later that day, I was rushed back into surgery for an emergency hysterectomy. Needless to say, Ryan's arrival definitely made an impact on us. It was a long day for Dan and a long recovery for me.

It wasn't only Ryan's delivery and my recovery that were difficult. Ryan was the opposite of Luke. While Luke was an easy baby, Ryan was not. His entire first year of life was difficult. We had many long nights walking the floors with a colicky or teething Ryan. It got so bad that there was a time when Luke spent every school night at Liz's house, so that he could get a good night's sleep for the next day. Some nights, Liz traded with us. She would walk Ryan and we would crash at her house. Working together, the three of us survived, and Ryan eventually learned to sleep through the night.

chapter 18

"Kris," Pastor Jon Green pokes his head into our gathering in Liz's room. "Would you mind waking Jenny for me? I'd like to spend a few minutes talking with her."

"No problem," I smile at Liz's obviously questioning eyes.

"Remember," I say to her, standing up alongside her bed, "no questions."

"Humphf" is the muffled reply I hear, as I join Jon in the hallway.

"Are you willing to do this?" I ask quietly, hoping that I'm not overheard by Liz's curious ears.

"Yes," he responds with a smile. "I'm impressed with Mike's love for both Liz and Jenny. I'm glad I can be here to witness this. If Jenny agrees, she and Mike can get the license as soon as the courthouse opens and I will sign it then. Since it is now November

11, we won't be lying when we say they were married on 11/11."

"11/11... I didn't realize," I say. "Should I tell Jenny why I'm waking her up or just let you talk to her?"

"Actually, if you could send her to the living room, Mike wants to propose the idea first," Jon answers.

"Ok, I'm sure she will be right out," I grin, stepping into the lower level guest room.

"Is it Mom?" Jenny startles, hearing me come in.

"No, honey, she's okay right now. It's Mike. He'd like to see you in the living room," I answer.

Jenny quietly walks out of the room. I realize that though she slept, she hardly rested. Perhaps we all look as extremely exhausted as she does. Walking back into Liz's room I wonder if I will ever feel rested again. How does one recover when faced with the new reality of living and breathing without the company of your kindred spirit? How will I do this?

I can hear the murmurs from the living room. My heart swells with love for Mike and for this extended family that envelopes me.

"Is she going for it?" Dan whispers to me, as I step into Liz's room.

"I'm going out to find out," Mark jumps up when I shrug my shoulders.

"And, I'm coming with you!" Luke softly exclaims.

"Wah?" Liz asks, trying to sit up.

"Sit tight, Lizzie," Dan says, walking to stand by her. "I promise all will be revealed in due time," he says in his best game show host voice.

I walk to the other side of her bed and she relaxes back into her pillow.

"Want to try another sip?" I ask.

She nods and I offer her the straw. Swallowing is becoming more and more difficult. Dan gently wipes what doesn't make it down. Seeing his gentle touch burns my throat. I think of all the times I have taken him for granted and the burning increases. Who am I to be so blessed?

~*~

The years in the cul-de-sac houses flew by. Our days were filled with school events, sporting events, and church events. Those day-to-day moments, that went unnoticed at the time, are now what we recall, counting them as gifts.

"Now what do I do?" she contemplated, on the way home from the bus stop on a cool October morning. With Jenny in school full day, Liz found herself lacking purpose.

"What do you mean?" I asked, pulling Ryan in the wagon.

"You still have Ryan home," she said. "I have nothing to fill my time while the kids are in school."

"Do you want Ryan?" I laughed. "I could take on a lot more freelance jobs if you do."

"See," she started. "That's just it. You take on freelance jobs. You create book illustrations and cover art. You have Ryan to keep you company. You have purpose."

"And, you feel like you have none," I said, beginning to understand.

"No," she replied, "it's not that bad! I do feel as if I have less purpose, though. I need something to do. I need to be needed."

"What about your music?" I asked.

"What music?" she countered. "I only ever play for myself or for you guys. It's not like I write music or anything."

"Why not?"

"Why not, what?" she questioned.

"Write music," I replied.

"For whom?" she doubted.

"For whomever will listen," I stated. "You have extreme talent. Why don't you share that talent with the world?" For a while we walked in silence. I pulled Ryan's wagon and Liz contemplated my idea.

"How do I do that?" she asked, finally.

"I don't know, exactly," I replied, "but, we can find out."

For the next few days, I contacted associates of the publishing world. My years of freelance work had introduced me to all sorts of people in the art world from corporate executives to college interns. Fortunately, for Liz, the art world is intertwined with the music world and after only a couple of days, I found an agent willing to listen to Liz's demo.

"You are such a good friend," she said when I told her. "This sounds perfect. And, it probably would be perfect... if I had a demo!"

"Calm down, Friend," I replied with a grin. "It's all good! Just call Dr. Ruflogel. I'm sure he has never forgotten you. I am equally sure he would love to help. Don't forget, the production students are always looking for practice in the campus recording studio."

"Have I told you, lately," she declared, giddily, "that you are a genius?"

"It's an understood fact," I retorted. "No need to say it again."

By the end of the week, Liz had a meeting scheduled with Dr. Alan Ruflogel, Chair of the Music Department of the university. A twenty minute drive was all it took for Liz to be back on campus and in the office of her old music department acquaintance.

"How can I help you, Liz?" Dr. Ruflogel asked, after a few minutes of small talk.

With as much of the "Old Liz Moxie" as she could muster, Liz pitched herself to Dr. Ruflogel. She mentioned that she had an agent waiting for a demo and offered herself as practice for the music production students. She volunteered to pay the studio fee. She not only asked for access to a piano, she also asked to use one of the university's harps. Even before Liz finished her plea, Dr. Ruflogel agreed to every single request.

"How soon do you want the studio?" he smiled.

"How soon can I get it?" she replied.

Dr. Ruflogel made a few phone calls and scheduled Liz for two hours in the recording studio that very afternoon. He also gave her keys to a piano practice room and a harp practice room.

"Do you mind if I observe your recording?" he asked, offering her the keys and his hand.

"After all that you are doing for me, how could I refuse?" she answered, shaking his hand.

"Fine," he replied. "Bring these keys with you to the studio and I will get them there."

"Thank you, Dr Ruflogel!" Liz smiled. "Thanks for believing in me!"

"I am quite confident it will be my pleasure," he said, showing her to the door.

Liz hurried to the practice facility and lost herself in her own music until her appointment time. She played the classics, her own original compositions, and even extemporaneous music, as she enjoyed the moment. All too soon, it was time. Steeling herself against the notorious butterflies flapping deep within her, she walked into the studio and introduced herself. Two hours later, she walked out with three CDs and a profound sense of accomplishment.

It was the waiting to hear back from Liz's agent that just about drove her crazy.

chapter 19

She smiles. I know she is smiling because the conversation in the living room is currently driving her crazy.

“Mama,” Jenny says softly. Holding hands, she and Mike approach Liz's bed.

“Let me,” Mike whispers, softly kissing Jenny's cheek.

“Liz,” Mike begins. “I would like to ask for your daughter's hand in marriage.”

Liz turns to Mike and looks at him quizzically. Fully aware that she gave consent last summer, she does not follow Mike's request.

“Now, Mama,” Jenny announces. “Right here, right now, with you.”

Tears fill Liz's eyes. She looks at Jenny. She looks at Mike. She looks at Dan and she looks at me.

"Jon?" she asks me.

"Yes." I say. "This is why Jon is here."

"No," she shakes her head looking back at Mike. Mike and Jenny stand beside her stunned. They never thought she would say "no." In the doorway, Jon, Mark, and Luke all look confused.

"Why don't we all go refill our coffee," Dan gently says, ushering everyone, except me, out of the room. A quiet look of understanding passes between us. He understands his role in this situation and I appreciate mine. This isn't the first time I have interfered with Liz's parenting style. Though, I would argue that she has interfered with mine more over the years.

"Liz," I start, when the room is empty.

"No," came her quiet, but emphatic reply.

"Why?" I ask.

"Summer... dress... fun," she states. "Not. Like. This."

"Kind of selfish, don't you think?" I retort. She shoots me a dirty look.

"Don't start with me," I answer her look. "You have controlled much. You can not control how Mark and Jenny grieve when you're gone, though. Furthermore, you can not control how they are grieving now. Jenny needs this moment. This memory. This gift of you seeing her marry Mike. Mike recognizes this. On his own accord, he asked my opinion and then called Jon."

The tears that began falling when Mike first asked Liz, spill over and slide down her cheeks. With all the energy she can muster she adamantly shakes her head.

“Fine, be that way,” I say getting up. “I will go tell Mike and Jenny that they can't get married here tonight because Jenny's mom can't bear to think that her daughter won't have the quintessential fairy tale wedding.”

Standing next to her bed for a moment, I continue honestly.

“If I recall, the fairy tale wedding didn't do you much good. However, if that is what is most important to you, I will see that Jenny has the biggest and fanciest Cinderella ball in May. I will not, though, prohibit them from marrying tonight. Mike is the real deal, Liz, and giving Jenny this gift of marrying while her mother is still breathing is the greatest gift he could give her. I'm just sorry you won't see it.” Without another word, I walk out of Liz's room.

“I can NOT believe that Liz turned Mike down,” I say to Dan in the kitchen. “I am well aware that she is dying. However, even in her death she can really tick me off! How dare she steal this moment from Jenny?”

“Kris,” Dan embraces me. “Don't waste these last moments angry. I'll go to Liz.”

Handing me his hot coffee, he turns to Liz's room. I am left standing holding a warm mug and wondering how Dan will patch this one over. Once again, my mouth got the better of me and Dan was left to pick up my pieces. He's had much practice over the years.

"Jenny. Mike," Dan calls. We all start toward Liz's room and Jon stops us.

"I think he just called Mike and Jenny," Jon says, putting his arm around me. He is one of my favorite people. In just the few years that Dan, Liz, and I have lived here at the Estate, Pastor Jon Green and his wife, Cathy, have become some of our dearest friends. They have blessed us abundantly and have made the gratitude list often.

"Thanks for being here," I mention. "This is so hard. Honestly, I can't believe I just spoke to Liz that way."

"Knowing Liz the way I do," he laughs, "it may have been your only option. Besides, she knows your heart. Just remember, she only wants the best for Jenny."

"I know," I reply. "She's always wanted the best. I guess, though, she forgot that a fairy tale wedding here at the Estate does not equal happily ever after."

"Who's to say that wedding here tonight is not a fairy tale?" Jon asks, and I laugh out loud. "Just because she doesn't share her Mom's idea of a fairy tale does not mean that this won't be Jenny's fairy tale dream."

"Wisely stated," Dan says, overhearing our conversation. "That is the same idea Liz and I just discussed."

"Discussed?" I ask, sceptically.

"Well, I discussed," he replies, "and she agreed."

"I'm so glad we both have you," I say, hugging the man who continues to live the fairy tale with me. "You are amazing."

"Looks like we're having a wedding," Jon comments, seeing Mike and Jenny come to the living room with wide smiles.

"Thanks, Kris," Liz croaks, as Dan and I walk back into her room.

"You're welcome, of course," I say, reaching down to kiss her cheek. "It's only 'cause I love you, you know."

"I know," she says.

I wipe her eyes and Dan holds her while I fluff her pillows. When Liz is comfortable again, we all gather around her. With Pastor Jon Green officiating, and in the presence of her mother, Jenny lives her fairy tale. She becomes Mrs. Micah Caldwell and the first person to congratulate her is her mom.

"Love you," Liz says, as first Jenny and then Mike lean down to kiss her.

"Love you too, Mama," Jenny says. "Thank you for giving up your dream for mine."

There isn't a dry eye in the entire room.

~*~

Liz's song-writing career didn't take off in the traditional sense that music legends are born. Instead of being "discovered" by a big name production company, she was hired by an advertising firm to write the music for commercial jingles.

"I don't care!" she exclaimed. "I'm writing music!"

It became obvious to all involved that Liz was not in it for the money. It's a good thing she wasn't. The monetary pay was pittance. The reward of doing what she loved was priceless. During the day, while Mark and Jenny were in school, Liz would write music. She had the Christmas harp moved from the Estate to her home. When it arrived, she turned her formal dining room into a music room. She gave her buffet, dining table, and chairs to a family at church. She and the kids ate all their meals sitting on stools at the kitchen counter. When she wanted to have a formal meal, it was at my house.

Liz's agent kept her busy. Before long, she was writing more than just jingles. She began working with Hollywood music directors writing scores for motion pictures. She took her work seriously, sometimes losing herself in her music. There were days she would forget to shower and eat before the kids got off the bus. She had purpose. She was happy.

"Happiness is overrated," she told me later, when we were counting gifts. "I was happy but I was also at peace. I think if I wouldn't have been, I couldn't have dealt with the diagnosis."

Part of Liz's follow up cancer treatment was a mammogram

once every six months. Initially, she dreaded the appointment and the stress of waiting for the results. Over time, though, she relaxed. Until, the phone call jolted her.

"Mrs. Bower, we need to schedule an ultrasound for you. We have a suspicious reading on your mammogram from this morning," the hospital clerk said pleasantly over the phone.

"Oh!" Liz heard her own shocked voice, but didn't recall speaking. "Ok, when?"

"We have you scheduled for tomorrow morning at 8:30. Please check in with the registration desk when you get here. After they take your insurance information, they will escort you to our radiology department," she continued in the same pleasant phone voice.

"Ummmm... ok," Liz stammered.

"We will see you then. Have a good day. Good-bye," and with that, the pleasant phone voice hung up.

"Kris," she called me, in a voice much more frantic than pleasant. "There's something suspicious."

"What?" I asked, incredulously. "Where?"

"In the remaining breast," she choked.

"Hold on! I will be right there," I shouted into the phone. Simultaneously, I slipped my feet in to my boots, grabbed Ryan's boots and coat, and interrupted his Sesame Street show.

"You can watch it at Aunt Liz's," I said, shoving his arms into

his coat sleeves. "If we hurry, you won't miss much of it." I literally ran him out the door.

The next day, I found a sitter for Ryan and went with Liz to the ultrasound appointment. The entire experience was surreal. We had been here before. Instead of blissful ignorance, though, we knew what to expect. None of it was new. By the end of the day, chemo and radiation were discussed and surgery was scheduled. We left the oncologist's office exhausted.

"I don't want to do this again," Liz confessed on the way home.

"Me, neither," I replied.

"I can't run away to the Estate this time," she said. "I can't pull the kids out of school. I can't take Mark out of basketball and take Jenny away from her friends."

"But, you want to go," I finished for her.

"Yes, but what I want doesn't really matter," she replied quietly. "Do you suppose a One-Breasted Wonder can still be a wonder if she is breast-less?"

"Knowing this Wonder, I know she can," I answered, reaching over to squeeze her hand. "Let's call Dr. Newhart and ask him to postpone your surgery for one week. We can take the kids out of school for a week and go to the Estate. We could all use a mid-winter break. I'm sure it's beautiful, all covered with snow."

"What about Dan?" she asked.

"Don't worry about Dan. I'll take care of getting him to join us," I smiled. "Although, he's more likely to say 'yes' if you ask."

By the end of the evening, all plans were made. Dan's colleague graciously covered Dan's appointments as well as his own. Dr. Newhart agreed that a vacation before surgery and chemo would do wonders for his patient. The kids excitedly packed their bags. We left early the next morning and we returned ten days later refreshed. We spent our week playing hard and having incredible fun in the snow. We introduced the kids to tobogganing, cross-country skiing, and downhill skiing. We made snow angels and built snowmen. An epic snowball fight happened on the last day we were there. Papa and Jenny buried Mark and Luke in snowballs. The healing balm of the Estate soothed again. Liz came home ready to take on another round of chemotherapy.

"He says I'm healing slower because I'm older," Liz moaned, when I asked two weeks later how she was feeling. "Getting older stinks."

"Sure does, Friend," I laughed, as she sat in her rocking chair and I cleaned her house.

Liz's recovery from surgery, the second time around, was twice as long and twice as hard. Her first chemo treatment came before she was fully recovered. Though she was older and slower to heal, the advancement of medicine in the years between her chemo treatments improved immensely. New drugs had been developed and tested to reduce the side effects of chemotherapy. The new anti-nausea drugs helped considerably.

"I donated all my old scarves to the cancer support group when my hair grew back in last time. Want to go shopping?" she called one morning.

"Sure. Today?" I asked.

"Yep, gotta hurry. Hair started falling out in the shower this morning. It seems to be falling out faster than last time. It almost clogged the shower drain," she commented. "What time can you be ready to go?"

Advancement in medicine wasn't the only change I noticed. Liz had changed too. No longer worried about fashion, she chose a variety of hats this time around. We laughed and giggled our way through the mall trying on every single hat we could find. For the afternoon, having fun was all that mattered, and for the moment we pretended we were eighteen again.

"Would you want to be eighteen again?" I asked Liz soberly.

"Not on your life!" she blurted. "We might not be as young and as beautiful as we were then but we certainly are wiser!"

I looked at Liz and was sure she was more beautiful now, hair falling out and all, than she was those years ago when we thought we could take on the world.

"Hey!" I yelled laughing. "Who's not as beautiful? I'm sporting beautiful abdominal stripes that I didn't have before and o are you. They're beauty marks, you know!"

"Stretch marks and scars... battle wounds of motherhood, cancer, and aging," she answered. "We wear them with pride!"

In that moment, I finally realized that attractiveness is more than beautiful hair and thin legs, and beauty is more than smooth skin. On this day, I not only saw Liz as being beautiful, I saw beauty in myself. It would be a while, though, before Liz would embrace that lesson. Together, we were a knock-out pair. Jauntily sporting hats, we left the mall for a quieter place to eat lunch.

Laughter and life lessons... beautiful gifts.

chapter 20

Jenny's and Mike's wedding reception consists of all of us gathering around Liz's bed smiling and wiping tears. Joy and sorrow mingle together. Thankfully, Luke has the presence of mind to snap picture after picture with my camera. The same camera that hasn't left this room in the past week. Digital images of my poor attempt at capturing time. A memory card filling up with glimpses of last memories. By the time I upload and print the images, photos will be all that we have.

I see a flash as Jenny, Mike, and Mark pose with Liz. My heart catches. This moment, it is all we have left. Liz, hardly living, is propped up with pillows. Her too thin frame outlined under the blankets that have her tucked in. I close my eyes and let my other senses take over. Somehow trying to burn this memory to my mind forever. The sounds of soft laughter and quiet voices.

The faint smell of Liz's perfume. The feel of family surrounding her. The taste of my salty tears. All of these are details that a flash and a camera cannot capture.

Jon hugs Jenny and shakes Mike's hand. He has accomplished what he came for. After a few hours of rest, Mike and Jenny will find him with the license and he will make it official. He kneels low and prays with Liz, one last time. I cannot help it. I nod to Luke, silently asking him to take this picture as well. I will need it. I know.

Dan sees Jon to the back door where he gathers his umbrella, boots, and coat. With a long hug and a promise to continue praying, he leaves for home in the dark of night. It is so very dark and so very cold. Dan watches the tail lights fade. I watch Dan.

The impromptu wedding has lightened the mood. Everything is different now, though nothing has really changed. Luke, Mark, and Mike refill coffee cups and settle down in the living room with a movie. Jenny joins in, snuggling deep into Mike's shoulder. Within minutes, she is fast asleep. Jana cleans the kitchen, again. Dan dons his boots and coat for a quick stretch outside. Though everyone is still here, still waiting, it seems as if they are no longer watching.

I turn back to Liz's room. I will watch. I need to watch. She smiles and closes her eyes. Deep fatigue is reflected in her smile. Deep fatigue and a deeper sense of peace. For the first time in ten days, since Hospice came to this Estate... this room... she is at peace. When I sense her peace, I begin to panic.

"Don't," she rasps.

"Don't what?" I whisper. "Don't notice your peace? Don't worry? Don't panic?" I say this louder than I realize.

"No fear, only peace," she quietly breathes.

"I know," I say. "I know. It's because you no longer fear that I am afraid. I fear what is coming. I fear the unknown. I fear breathing without you. I fear living again." I taste bitter, salty tears. There is no answer this time. At some point in my pity party, she has fallen asleep. I watch her chest, wanting to see it rise and fall. I'm not disappointed. She simply sleeps.

I wait and watch, alone.

~*~

Liz weathered the remainder of the chemo amazingly well. She told people it was because she had such a great housekeeper and incredibly clean toilets. Though most people laughed, some took her seriously. I simply rolled my eyes. It was her sense of humor, her music, and her love for God that got her through. Though, not necessarily in that order.

"I cannot believe it!" she exclaimed, looking over my shoulder. Liz often walked right into our house without knocking.

"What?" I questioned, looking up from the astronomy textbook cover design that I was working on.

"That!" she said, looking at my work. "I cannot believe you do that!"

"Just as I cannot believe the music you write," I countered. "Now, I know that isn't what you came over here to tell me. What is it that you cannot believe?"

"This!" she cried, ripping off her hat. I was stunned. There were no words. I wanted to laugh and Liz wanted to cry.

"Well, the good news is that your hair is growing back," I stammered.

"And, the bad news is that I am completely gray," she whimpered. "Gray. Old woman gray." Having said that, she donned her hat, turned around, and walked back out my front door.

When Liz's hair grew back after her first chemotherapy, she had soft, glamourous curls. She kept her hair short and sported the curls beautifully. This time age worked against her hair. Instead of soft curls, she had coarse, straight, gray hair. We tried everything to cover her gray. After three different boxes of hair color, we called Liz's favorite hair stylist. Carrie tried a few of the tricks up her sleeve. However, when those failed, she sat Liz down and broke the news to her.

"Liz, you are healthy and beautiful, and you are gray.

Embrace it. Fighting it will do you no good. The way your hair is now, it simply will not take a color," she said as gently as she could. Liz cried all the way home.

"Who am I?" she sobbed in the seat next to me.

"What do you mean, 'who are you'?" I asked. "You are Elizabeth Bower, of course."

"No," she sniffed. "I know that. It's when I look in the mirror that I don't know who I am."

"What?" I asked quietly. "What do you mean?"

"Kris," she began. "How much has your body changed in the past twenty years?"

"Well, aside from the zebra-like stripes that I sport thanks to Ryan, the extra ten pounds I carry around, and the fact that everything seems to be sagging, I guess it's about the same," I answer, trying to encourage her with a little humor.

"Trade you," she said, quietly.

"Sure," I replied. "I'll trade you any day. You are tall, thin, and stunningly beautiful!"

For a time, she stared out the passenger car window at the scenery passing by. I glanced at her several times and watched the silent tears fall. Not knowing what to say, I wisely stayed quiet.

"I've lost my breasts, one at a time. In their place, I now have scars. One red, one white. I've lost my hair twice. In its place, I

have hair twenty-five years older than I am. I have two tattoos on my bare chest from radiation. I am legally married to a man who has left me, never to return. I wear a ring to remind me daily of a commitment I made years ago, and it reminds me of my own violation of that covenant. I look in the mirror and wonder where the woman of twenty years ago went and I loathe the woman who stares back at me," she finally replied.

"But, Liz," I began, "you are so beautiful!"

"Kris, stop!" she ordered. "Until you have both of your saggy breasts chopped off one at a time, and you've lost your hair twice and it grows back ugly gray, do not patronize me!"

"Um, okay, sorry!" I said quietly.

I could probably count on one hand the number of times Liz raised her voice at me. This time surprised me most. Neither of us said another word. When we pulled into my driveway, Liz got out, slammed the door, and stomped across the street to her house.

Honestly, Liz was right on with what she said. How could I presume to understand what she was feeling? While I did lose my uterus after Ryan's birth, few people knew it. I didn't lose the external evidence of my femininity. Though saggy and stripy, my body more closely resembles the body I wore twenty years ago, than hers does. My hair has only a little gray. I wouldn't be mistaken as anyone's grandmother. I couldn't say the same for Liz.

I desperately wanted Liz to see what we all saw, a woman

more beautiful now than she was at age eighteen. I wanted her to see the woman of grace, of joy, of inner beauty that I call my friend. I was at a loss as to how to do this. She was obviously shutting me out. This was an inner pain that she would not share. So, I prayed.

The next day, Liz acted as if nothing had happened, so I played along.... for a little while.

"Liz, come here," I said a few days later.

"Where are you?" she asked.

"In my room," I answered, standing in front of my full length mirror. When Liz joined me, I positioned her in front of me.

"Do you know what I see here?" I asked.

"Kris, don't," she mumbled.

"No, Liz, I must," I replied. "I must say this once. If you choose to ignore me or to not believe me, that is your prerogative. My heart must voice this and I ask you to listen this once."

Liz looked to the floor. She said nothing, so I continued, "You are the most beautiful woman I know. I see courage and endurance in you. You wear the beauty of laughter around your eyes and an engaging smile on your face. I see a woman who lives by Truth and is true to her commitments. You stand tall and straight with an elegance gleaned from years of life. You move with a regal grace. Your heart is full of love and mercy and you use your hands to help others. I see a mother who wants only the best for her children and a friend who is the sister I longed for. Elizabeth, you are beautiful."

Liz said turned away without saying a word. She had made it perfectly clear that the matter was off limits. I continued to pray.

Now that she was well again, she jumped back into the music scene. Several producers had kindly waited while Liz underwent treatments. Once she was finished with her treatments, the same compassionate producers were impatiently anxious for Liz to write them a music score, or two. She was equally anxious to get back to creating. Her world, once again, became music and family.

Eventually, she apparently came to accept her new look. With short gray hair, I thought she was still stunningly beautiful. She simply looked like Mark and Jenny's grandmother instead of their mother.

"I guess I am now the Gray-Haired Wonder," she commented one day. "I only wish I could come up with a really great come-back to the unsolicited comments that I receive. If one more person refers to me as Jenny's grandmother, I am going to have a fit!"

"Just tell them you are her great-grandmother. They will think you are so young," I quipped back.

"Not funny!" she laughed anyway.

It did my heart good to hear that sound. God answers prayer in mysterious ways and no way more mysterious than the answer he brought to Liz.

chapter 21

Rob's conspicuously absent. It is not that he doesn't want to be here with us tonight. Rather, she asked him not to come. She said "good-bye" to him before Hospice came. She told him that she loved him, but these last days were for family, and she hoped he understood.

Though he doesn't understand, he loves her. So, he honors her wishes and calls Dan frequently for updates. Dan doesn't mind. They have forged a friendship over the last few years. These two men who love the same woman. He trusts that Dan will give him honest health reports and Dan respects him too much to lie. It is a good relationship.

"Do you think he should have been here?" I ask Dan, quietly.

"I don't think it matters much what I think," he replies thoughtfully. "I didn't have much say. It is Lizzie's decision and her choice."

"I know, but..." I say wistfully. "I wish he could be here. I wish it could be different. I wish it were different."

"If wishes were horses," Dan quotes the Mother Goose nursery rhyme, "beggars would ride."

"If turnips were swords, I'd have one by my side," I quote back. "I still wish he were here by her side."

"Sweetheart," Dan takes my hand gently, "wishing does no good. Lizzie and Rob, they've worked it out. It is what it is and it's good."

Looking at Dan, I sigh. I know he's right. I know my wishing doesn't change anything for Liz or for Rob or for any of us. Yet, my heart keeps on longing... yearning... dreaming. I think of "if only" a million and one times. I think of how different tonight might be if just one "if only" had happened.

Glancing at Liz, I am reminded that the time for wishes and dreams and "if only" is almost gone. It's been Liz who has reminded me that life is not a dress rehearsal and there is no second chance. And, though we may desire a different ending, we do not get to choose.

Instead, we live one life. And, to live it well, we gratefully count the gifts along the way. We cannot stop the hands of time. Instead, we can hold each moment. It is in each moment that we truly live. Liz knew this and lived each moment. She has taught me how.

"Have you talked to him recently?" I ask.

"By 'recently' do you mean tonight?" He teases. Dan and I have an inside joke that "recent" has a different meaning to each of us. My recent is much more current than his.

"Yes," I say quietly.

"I spoke to him while I walked outside to stretch. Rob's concerned and he's praying. He understands her enough to honor her wishes and loves her enough to allow us these last moments with her."

"He really is an incredible guy," I murmur. "I wish they could have been together."

"There you go wishing again," Dan quietly teases, pulling me to him again. "Let them have what they have. It works for them and they have been happy together."

I nod my head against his chest. Once again, this wise man I have spent my life with is right and I am wrong. He and I, we have had decades to be happy together. She and Rob, they have had a few years. Different but good... gifts.

~*~

"He found me," she said sitting down on the other one of my front porch rockers.

"Who did? Robert?" I asked.

I had been enjoying the cool evening air on the porch while Dan was with the kids at one of the many ballgames he attended each spring. It was Ryan's Little League game tonight. Dan was Ryan's assistant Little League coach and Luke was working my shift at the concession stand. Dan took Mark and Jenny along as well. They were all proud of themselves for finding a way to give Liz and me a night off. We were thrilled to enjoy it.

"No. Yes." she said, almost imperceptibly, while sipping her iced tea.

"Did you say 'no' or 'yes'," I asked.

"Both," she said, slightly louder, looking at me with large eyes and a solemn face.

"Liz," I pleaded, "help me here. Is Robert here?"

"No," she started, "Dr. Robert Bower is not here and I have no idea where he is. I just spent twenty minutes talking with Robert Adams on the phone."

"Who is Robert Adams?" I asked, more confused than ever.

"Robert Adams is a music producer in Nashville. He found me through an old jingle that I had written and got in touch with my agent. His message with my agent was that he was looking for someone to write the music for an up and coming artist in Nashville."

"Since when do you do country music songs?" I interrupted.

"I don't," she continued. "Apparently, though, I live them. When I called him back, I heard his voice. Rob found me."

"Rob?!" I asked incredulously. "Rob from a long time ago, Rob? The one from the music department's faculty summer recital? That Rob?"

"Yes," she murmured.

"Well," I yelled, jumping out of my chair, "what did he say?"

"He apologized. He said he's been looking for me for ten years to tell me he was sorry."

"Wow!" I exclaimed. "What prompted that?"

"I don't know. He didn't say and I didn't think to ask."

"Is he married?" I asked, thoughtfully.

"Does it matter?" she asked back, looking straight through me. "I am. It does not matter if he is married or isn't married."

"Well," I hesitated, "I was just wondering why he worked so hard to find you. I know you said to apologize. Could it be he's thinking something else?"

"I don't know what he's thinking," she commented.

"So," I pressed, "is that all there was, just an apology?"

"And lunch tomorrow."

Rob came to town the next day specifically to make that lunch date. Wouldn't I have loved to be a fly on the wall in that bistro? Liz later confided that she was grateful for that extremely awkward luncheon.

"Closure," she subsequently said. "I didn't realize how much I needed the closure. I needed the opportunity to tell Rob how much I struggled after that night and how sorry I was. I needed to tell him about Jenny and how she is Robert's daughter. More than anything, I needed to tell him it was my fault. I was a bit like Potiphar's wife pursuing Joseph. Rob's only shortcoming was that, unlike Joseph, he didn't leave his coat behind. I am so thankful that God granted me the chance to look Rob in the eye and apologize. For that, and for his forgiveness, I am ever so grateful we met for that appointment."

Liz always refused to call it a date. She told Rob all about her renewed commitment to her marriage vow and Robert's disappearance. When Rob offered to pay for her lunch, she refused. She violated her marriage vow once, she wouldn't do it again. At the end of their hour lunch, Rob asked if he could contact her again. She didn't answer. She simply paid her bill and walked out leaving Rob alone at the table.

I laugh now, looking back. Liz finally met her match of tenacity in Rob. As tenacious as she was about her marriage, he pursued a friendship with her more. He pushed enough, without pushing her away. Amazingly, in the end, it was Rob's platonic love that healed Liz's heart. In his pursuit of her, she recognized her beauty and finally accepted her scars, her gray hair, and her flat chest as parts of a whole beautiful person.

I don't know when that happened for Liz. I'm not sure she does either. Perhaps it was Rob's gentle faithfulness or the fact that he always sent a bouquet with calla lilies for her birthday. Maybe it was that he never called her by her given name. Instead, he always referred to her as "Beautiful." Maybe it was the fact that he once saw her in what she thinks of as her "beautiful body" and now loves her for her beautiful soul. Whatever it was, she eventually buried the severe hatred she had of herself and embraced a God-honoring friendship with a man she once knew.

The beauty of their relationship is that they never required anything of the other. It wasn't until this summer that Liz ever learned Rob's life story. After pursuing her for years, he finally trusted her enough to gift her with the telling of it.

chapter 22

"Over these last few years, Liz and Rob have developed a deep friendship. He calls and emails and she calls and writes back. A few times a year, Rob will come here to visit. He always stays with us and Liz visits him at our house. It has done my heart good to watch them become friends. Good friends," I say to Liz's nurse, Jana.

"I find it amazing that he came back for her after all those years," Jana quietly replies. "What took him so long?"

"Pain," I respond. "Deep pain that renders one's heart paralyzed for a time."

"Because of that night with Mom?" Jenny asks, quietly.

"So deep was I in the telling of the story," I say, smiling at Jenny, "I didn't realize you came back into the room."

"Mike's asleep. He had a busy shift. I left him sleeping on the couch and came back in for more of the story," she answers.

"Did Mom cause Rob's deep pain?" Jenny asks again.

"No," I reply, thoughtfully. Rob has since shared his pain with Dan and me. It's his story, though. I don't know how much to share with Jenny.

"Jenny," Dan interjects. "I think you and Mike should take a weekend to visit Rob in Nashville. He has a beautiful home in the Tennessee mountains. Not only would he appreciate your company, but if you ask, I'm confident he will tell you his story."

"But, you won't tell me now," she smiles.

"It's not my story to tell," he replies. "I will say this, though, a visit to Rob is always worth the drive. He is an incredible host, his property is stunning, and his story is an amazing testimony of love and redemption."

"Ok, Uncle Dan," Jenny says, laughing quietly, "I won't ask again."

"Life is pain," Jana remarks. "It's what we allow God to do with our pain that makes all the difference in our lives. I don't have to hear Rob's story to understand that he has surrendered his pain and allowed God to heal him and use him."

"That is exactly what he has done," I say, quietly. No one responds and we return to comfortable silence.

Right now... in this moment... I am moved beyond words. We are all here, those who love Liz. Yet, we are not all here. Rob and

Robert are not here. One by choice, the other by request. Ryan and Mom Murphy are not here either, though both have been here this week. Ash, Bea, Dad, and Joy are not with us, having gone on before. I am moved that Liz has family on both sides of this thing called death. We gather here to love on her until her last breath and those who have gone ahead wait on the other side to welcome her to eternity.

In the silence, I wonder what everyone is thinking and even more how we will each handle this imminent death. Liz's death. We've each known her in a different way and we each love her accordingly. Though I often worry about how difficult this will be for myself, I know it will not be easy for any of us. We will all struggle. We will all question. We will all hurt. There is pain in death. I am confident of this... there are also gifts.

~*~

Life has a way of ebbing and flowing. Thankfully, it is neither always frantic, nor is it always boring. Each stage, each season, has its own problems and pleasures. Some would say that no season has more problems than the season of raising teenagers. Sometimes the problems outweigh the pleasures. Perhaps no one would agree more than Liz.

Amazingly, Liz never heard from Robert over the years. She neither tried to find him nor hide from him. She simply embraced life and raised her children on her own. Though the kids would sometimes ask about Robert, they never asked for him. To those standing on the fringe, Mark and Jenny seemed to be well-adjusted and happy children. Unfortunately, sometimes what cannot be seen is what simmers under the surface.

Mark entered high school as a freshman when he was fourteen. Though in his younger years he had been loving and kind, at fourteen he seemed to morph into a teenage tyrant. He no longer had patience for Jenny, Luke, or Ryan. He seemed to have little respect for Liz and absolutely no respect for the father who left. The one who had never returned. Thankfully, Liz recognized Mark's inner struggle. Though she felt like a failure as a mother, she prayed for him continually.

Football was Mark's love. He spent every waking moment dreaming of football, and every night his sleep would be filled with those dreams. Each day he spent his energy on the field, often taking out his heart frustrations on his own teammates. Every single day he ran extra laps at the end of practice as punishment for his lack of self-control.

"Mark," Coach Tom Zeller called. He approached as Mark finished his last discipline lap for a hard late hit during practice. "Mark, you are one of the most talented players on my team. You have incredible potential. You also have incredible anger. If you

can't get a hold of your anger and exercise some self-control, I will have no choice but to sideline you for Saturday's game. I can't afford the penalty yards you could cost us. However, there is a starting right guard position with your name on it. The choice is yours."

"OK, Coach," Mark mumbled, while catching his breath. "I hear you."

"Alright then," Coach smiled. "I'll see you on the starting roster."

Coach Tom Zeller was a gem of a coach. He loved the game of football and he loved coaching junior varsity. He approached each season with the enthusiasm of an NFL coach. He believed every one of his young players had the potential to be the best football player ever. His enthusiasm was contagious. If enthusiasm won football games, Coach Zeller would have been undefeated. Tom also had a heart for kids. He quickly recognized the hurting child in Mark.

Mark's junior varsity home opener fell on a beautiful August day. A day that was also over ninety degrees. It was a hot one. The coaches had extra fluids on the sidelines and did their best to rotate the players, so that no one player suffered heat exhaustion. Before the coin toss, though, everyone was soaking wet. I couldn't imagine how hot it was inside those helmets.

We all sat in the bleachers, shading ourselves under big

umbrellas. The concession stand sold out of ice cream bars and popsicles before the end of the first quarter. They ran out of ice at half-time. Tempers flared. Looking back... maybe... just maybe... the heat was to blame for how things got out of control.

At half-time, we were down 14-3. The team huddled together under the bleachers to find some shade. Coach Zeller was patient. He knew his players were hot. He encouraged them to drink their Gatorade slowly and to sit still. He wanted them to reserve some energy for the last two quarters of play.

It was when they walked around the bleachers to go back to the field for the third quarter that Mark saw him... his father, or so he thought. To this day, none of us, including Mark, knows who he really saw. On that hot Saturday morning, though, no one could have convinced Mark it wasn't Robert. So, as the team headed to the sidelines, Mark pushed past his teammates and ran toward the man walking out of the gate. By the time Mark got to the gate, the man was gone. Flustered and frustrated, Mark sprinted back to the sideline.

"Where'd you go?" Mark's teammate, Tim, asked.

"I thought I saw my dad," Mark replied.

"Thought you didn't have a dad," Tim taunted. "I heard he walked out on you. Must be he's a loser."

One taunt was all it took. All of Mark's pent up teenage anger came through in a left hook and a right jab. Before the whistle to start the third quarter, Mark knocked out his own teammate and was ejected from the game. He was escorted off the playing field by an assistant coach while the trainers cared for Tim. Tim left the game as well, with a broken jaw.

"What is he thinking?" Liz screeched, running down the bleachers.

"Liz," Dan caught up with her. "Let him go for now. He needs to face the consequences."

"But, Dan," she whipped around. "He needs me."

"Yes, he does," Dan held her shoulders. "He needs you desperately. Right now, though, the greater need is to let him face the music. He'll need you to help pick up the pieces later. Besides, the last I knew, they don't let moms into the locker room."

"Will you go?" she asked frantically.

"Only if they come and ask for me," Dan wisely replied. "He doesn't need a doctor. He needs a father. Right now, I am his physician. When he is ready and when he asks, I will gladly step into the father role for him. However, he must choose me."

Liz and Dan stood side by side as they watched Mark enter the school with the assistant coach. Tears streamed down Liz's face. She could no longer pretend to be both mother and father to her children. Mark was spinning out of control and she was powerless to help him. It was a very angry young man who exited shortly after. He said nothing to Liz as he got into the car and she had no idea what to say to him.

"Yes, this is Mrs. Bower," Liz said into the phone two days later.

"What?! I'm sorry, you will have to contact my attorney!" She hung the phone up and slid down the kitchen wall. The local newspaper called. Tim's family was suing. Because Mark had no previous juvenile record, they skipped criminal court. They opted, instead, to sue for damages in civil court. The reporter had called asking Liz to comment on the suit filed. Wisely, she said nothing.

When Mark came home from school, he found his mother still sitting against the wall on the kitchen floor. Her tears had dried, but her eyes were glazed. Instead stopping to tell her then that he had been kicked off the JV football team, Mark walked away and slammed his bedroom door. A framed sketch I had drawn for Liz, years before, fell to the floor and the glass shattered, much like Liz's heart.

chapter 23

"And, you saved me," Mark says quietly, looking straight at Dan.

"No," Dan answers, "Jesus saves, not me."

"OK," Mark smiles, "but you loved me for who I was and got me help when I needed it most."

"Dr. Chisham," Dan smiles back. "We were in medical school together. Even then, I knew she would be a great psychiatrist some day. The amazing thing about Sara is that she is not only a good doctor, she is an amazing counselor."

"The first few times I went, I hated it," Mark remembers. "The funny thing is that I thought I was so good at pretending. I still remember the day she looked right at me and said, 'you are mad that you are here,' and I thought she could read my mind!"

"No, I think she just read your eyes," Dan chuckles. "You

were walking around with a pretty big chip on your shoulder."

"I remember. I had to go once a week for twelve weeks according to the judge. I counted down thinking I couldn't wait to be done. After I finished my twelve weeks, though, I asked Mom if I could keep seeing Dr. Sara for a while. My appointments with her helped me understand why I hated my father. I went to her all through high school. She helped me a lot," Mark reminisces. "She even came to my high school graduation open house."

"I'm glad Judge Bruner asked for and used my recommendation as your primary care physician. Rather than punish you, he got you help. I'm also glad that Tim's family agreed to settle out of court for punitive damages, community service, and court-ordered help for you," Dan recalls. "You know, Sara later confided in me that you were one of her favorite patients."

"Yeah, and later Judge Bruner was instrumental in getting me another chance on the football team. He came to every single one of my varsity home games, and he let me work on the grounds crew for the school as my community service," Mark remembers. "I guess I was one of the lucky ones, he gave me another chance. A lot of people did, especially you."

"Blessed," Dan says. "Not lucky, blessed. We are all blessed. You earned that second chance. You worked hard."

"It was Dr. Sara who helped me realize that though I had a father, I needed and wanted a dad. Thanks for being my dad all these years," Mark says, quietly.

"It's been an honor and a privilege. Thanks for asking me," Dan answers. "I continue to pray for you, Son."

"I know," Mark whispers, watching Liz. "Many prayers have been said on my behalf. Thank you."

As I listen to these two talk around me, I watch Liz sleep. I wonder, again, what Liz hears in this twilight of her life. Can she hear us talk around her? Does she hear the testimony of God's grace? Does she know the answers to prayer? Can she hear all of us, her family, loving on each other as we gather around her?

We have talked much lately, she and I, about this incredible blended family that we have. It seems that the glue that has bonded us most is the living life together that we have done. We have upheld one another through the hard times. I sit next to her and wonder why the gifts in life are most often wrapped in hardship? And, why does it seem the best gifts come tied up in pain?

~*~

God's grace is evident every single day. We just have to look for it. Slowly, Liz began to see God's grace at work in Mark's heart. The weekly trips to Dr. Chisham's office became designated conversation time for Liz and her son. Though stilted at first, they both began to look forward to the forty minute drive time. Liz glimpsed her son's heart soften and he saw her sense of humor. Gradually, a relationship was redeemed. A grace gift.

Sensing that Mark was ready, Liz finally broached the subject of Rob. While she had been corresponding with Rob, and occasionally speaking with him on the phone, she had very much protected her children from any suspicion of a relationship. Dr. Sara, though, encouraged Liz to tell Mark about Rob. Perhaps Liz's honesty about Rob would help Mark trust her more.

"Mark," Liz began, while driving home from Mark's appointment. "I'd like to tell you about a friend I've made in the music world. His name is Rob."

"Rob?" Mark asked, hesitantly.

"Yes, but not Robert," Liz replied. "Actually, Rob and I met years ago. We have just lately become friends." While Liz told Mark about getting to know Rob, she did not tell him about how she first met Rob. Sometimes too much information is worse than not enough.

"Are you dating him?" Mark boldly asked.

"No, I am not," she replied. "But, I am glad you asked that. I've told Rob about Robert. I have made it clear to Rob that I am still married. He understands where I stand on that issue and he has agreed to respect my decision to stay married to your father. He also has agreed to be my friend. Rob is one of the few people I

know with whom I can discuss music and the music world. He understands me when I talk about my frustrations in writing a piece and he also understands my elation when I can record on paper the music that is in my heart. We are simply friends, Mark, nothing more."

"Friends like Uncle Dan?" Mark asked, quietly, trying to understand.

"No," Liz answered. "Your Uncle Dan is a very special man and a special friend. We've lived a lot of life together... Kris, Dan, and I. They are my best friends. Rob is simply a friend. I will never be as close to him as I am to Uncle Dan and Aunt Kris."

"Okay, I think I understand," Mark replied. "What exactly does Rob do in the music business?"

"He's a producer for some big names in Nashville. He's told me who he works with. I didn't recognize their names. Maybe you would though. He'd like to come here to meet you and Jenny. How do you feel about that?"

"I'm okay with that, Mom," Mark smiled. "I'd like to know who he works with. Maybe he could get some autographs for me!"

"Maybe he could, Mark," Liz smiled back. "Maybe he could."

"You know, Mom," Mark said, slyly, "it would be okay with me if you divorced Dad and dated Rob."

"Well," Liz replied, unsure of where this conversation was suddenly headed, "first of all, I feel strongly that I should be true to my word when I said 'until death do us part,' and secondly, who's to say Rob wants to date a woman with short gray hair that looks like your grandma?"

"Apparently he does," Mark laughed. "Isn't he the one that wants to come here, Grandma?"

"Good grief!" Liz exclaimed, enjoying Mark's laughter and joining with him.

Laughter... a gift for healing hearts.

chapter 24

I glance around. Everyone but Jana has nodded off for a few winks of sleep. “How do you stay awake,” I ask her quietly.

“I've worked this shift for so long, that even on my days off, my body doesn't sleep at nighttime. My preferred sleeping time is late morning until late afternoon,” she says from her corner chair.

“I doubt we have said it enough. Thank you for being here,” I say.

“You are welcome,” Jana replies. “My shift is almost finished. I'd like to stay, though, if it is okay with you and Liz's other family members.”

“Really?” I ask. “Why?”

“Well,” she begins, “I am enjoying this story and would love to hear it in its entirety. I also like being with your family. I would go home to an empty house this morning. It's warm and peaceful here."

"I know I speak for everyone when I say you are more than welcome to stay," I reply. "There are more bedrooms upstairs if you would like to lie down."

"I may take you up on that offer later this morning," she answers. "For now, though, I am very comfortable. I will help myself to anything I need. I think Becki is coming in this morning to work today's day shift."

"You know," I say, "we have been so blessed by incredible nurses for Liz. You have all been amazing."

Jana smiles at me and we sit quietly for a while. It seems to me that Liz's breathing has gotten raspier. I lean over and smooth her blankets... again. My heart is restless. I want to do something... anything... and there is nothing to do. I used to think I was a patient person, one who was good at waiting. Now, I know that isn't true, nor has it ever been. I was just really good at pretending.

"How long?" I quietly ask Jana, not sure I want the truth.

"Today," she whispers. My heart skips.

"And, this is why you want to stay?" I ask, hardly voicing the words.

"Yes," comes the hushed answer.

My throat burns and my heart hurts. I want to run, but where would I go when my heart is planted here? My pulse races at the thought of Liz's death and my breath comes fast. Here lies the dichotomy... Liz's heart slows and her breathing labors while I sit next to her with my racing heart breathing hard. I am not waiting well, as the morning light slips over the horizon.

"You mentioned earlier about a trip to Guatemala?" Jana asks, encouraging me to keep the story going. "When did that happen?"

Looking up I remember a brilliant sunset just north of the equator.

~*~

"I think I'd like to go to Guatemala," Dan stated one evening, while he and I cleaned up the kitchen after dinner. "There is a group of local physicians who go four times a year to offer free medical help to the local people there."

"Really?" I asked in response. Dan had never before mentioned any type of medical trip to another country. I wasn't sure if he was really serious. Then, again, Dan wasn't one to joke about helping others.

My husband was one of the most giving people I knew. He was quick to help others and rarely expected anything in return. His office gave to several charitable organizations. As a physician, he never turned someone down when they asked for help. He had never, before, gone out looking for someone to help, though. I didn't know what to make of my man's most recent announcement.

"When?" I asked, seeking more information.

"They leave in six weeks," Dan said slowly, bracing himself for my response, I'm sure.

"Six weeks?!" I sputtered, scrubbing the last pot in the sink. "Can you even get a passport in six weeks?"

"Yes," he answered. "Would you go with me?"

"Me?" I stammered. I couldn't believe he even asked me. Me, the one who chooses to drive because I hate to fly. Me, the one who has only ever flown twice in my entire life. Me, the one who has never been outside the borders of the United States, nor have I ever held a U.S. passport. He wanted me to go with him?

"The trip is eight days long," he said, laying down the dishtowel and wrapping his arms around me. "I'd hate to be away from you that long."

"But," I hesitated, "someone needs to stay here with the boys. It's Luke's senior year of high school. Ryan is still young. I'm not sure I want to leave him for that long, even with Liz."

"Well, you can't leave him with Liz," Dan said softly into my neck. "She and Jenny are going along."

"So, you are going?" I spun around and looked at him

sharply. "I thought you were asking if I minded if you went. Apparently, I don't have a say in this."

"Kris, stop!" Dan said, stepping away. Once again, my mouth got the best of me and ruined any moment we might have had.

"You do have a say. I haven't applied for a passport yet, and I haven't paid any money. I want to go on this trip, but I wanted to talk to you about it first. Are you willing to talk or are we going to argue?"

I once told Liz that one of the reasons I loved Dan was his uncanny ability to defuse just about every argument we ever had. I failed to mention that this very trait also drove me crazy.

"Fine," I said, slamming the towel on the counter. "Let's talk!"

"No," he said, walking away. "I will talk later."

"Ohhhhhhhhhh! You make me so mad!" I yelled to the back of the front door as he let himself out.

Hot tears streamed down my cheeks. He and Liz had made up their minds to go with or without me. I either had to do what they wanted or live eight days without them. I stomped off to my bedroom, slammed the door and threw myself face down on the bed.

Fifteen minutes later, I heard the door quietly open and close again. I assumed it was Dan coming back to "discuss" his upcoming trip, so I didn't move.

"Are you done throwing your fit?" Liz asked, with a smile in her voice.

"Go away," I mumbled into my pillow.

"Nope," she answered, sitting on the edge of my bed. "Not gonna do it."

I said nothing in reply, hoping that if I ignored her, she would leave me to my own pity party. I should have known better.

"Every party needs a pooper, that's why we invited you," Liz began to sing. "Party pooper! Party pooper!"

"Go away," I mumbled again.

"It's my party and I'll cry if I want to," she continued, switching songs and singing louder, "cry if I want to, cry if I want to."

"Out!" I yelled, rolling over and glaring at her.

"Oh, good," she smiled. "It worked!"

"Have I told you that I hate you," I scowled.

"Um," she said, thoughtfully, "not today."

"LIZ!" I yelled, "GET OUT!"

"I already told you that I can't do that," she replied.

"Why not?" I huffed.

"Because I cannot go to Guatemala without you," she softly

stated.

"I hate it when you and Dan gang up on me," I sniffed.

In the end, all six of us... Liz, Jenny, Luke, Ryan, Dan, and I went to the courthouse the next afternoon to apply for expedited passports. Mark had graduated from high school the year before and though he was invited to join us, he declined. Apparently, it was okay for him to decline... just not me.

The kids were thrilled with the prospect of adventure and going somewhere warm for spring break. Amazingly, Luke was the most excited of all.

"Going to Guatemala is way better than going to Florida for spring break, Mom!" he exclaimed.

Ultimately, even I got caught up in the excitement as the days flew by in a whirl-wind of preparations. And, before we knew it, it was the day of departure. We all got on the plane and I relaxed my white knuckle grip when we landed in Guatemala City. Had I known the gifts that were waiting, I might have enjoyed the flight.

chapter 25

"You were kind of funny, Mom," Luke laughs.

"I don't like to fly either," Jana states, encouraging me slightly. "I avoid it at all costs."

"I still don't really enjoy flying," I smile. "But, I've learned to relax a little and enjoy the ride."

"She still has white knuckles when she flies, Jana," Luke chuckles. "She just doesn't grit her teeth anymore."

"Hey!" I say, smiling at Luke, while looking at Jana. "Luke is right, though."

"I understand," Jana snickers.

"Really," Dan interjects, "she comes by it naturally. Her mom hates to fly as well."

"Is your mother still living?" Jana asks sweetly.

"She is," I reply. "She lives just down the road at Heritage

Lakes Retirement Community. She has a condo there and loves it."

"Didn't you say she lived here?" Jana asks.

"Yes," I answer. "She did live here for many years with Bea and Ash. Liz offered for her to stay when they passed away, but Mom said she didn't feel like that was right. I also think it was incredibly lonely here alone. She called us one day and told us she had moved to Heritage Lakes Community Center. We weren't too surprised. Mom developed quite a bit of independence when Dad died. After coming to visit, we realized why she chose Heritage Lakes. It is a wonderful community and she loves being around people."

"I visit Heritage Lakes often," Jana replies. "They have the most beautiful flower beds in the spring, summer, and early fall."

"Yes, they do," I smile. "Mom leads the volunteer group that oversees the flower beds. I will tell her you've noticed them. She will love knowing that someone appreciates them."

"Please do," Jana smiles back. "They really are beautiful gardens."

"Hello," Liz's next nurse, Becki, says as she steps into the room.

"Hi Becki," I answer.

"How is she?" Becki asks Jana.

"Her breathing is weakening. She's been unconscious for a

few hours now."

"OK," Becki answers. "I'm ready to take over."

"You're welcome to take over her care," Jana says, with an appreciative smile to me. "I'm going to stay though. Kris says she doesn't mind."

"I don't mind," I reiterate. "We are blessed to have both of you."

"I'll go finish my charting and give you her history," Jana says, walking toward the door. "If you'll sign it for me, Becki, then my shift will be officially finished."

"Sure," Becki replies, following her to the kitchen.

Watching Liz's nurses walk out, I look toward the kitchen window. I'm startled by the amount of daylight. Even with the continued rain, the kitchen is bathed in gray light. I am moved that our planet continues its rotation around the sun regardless of my pain. While the sun is setting on Liz's life, those of us living face a brand new day. Whether we want to or not.

"Jenny's asleep," Mike pokes his head in to tell me. "I'm going home to shower and change. I will be back to take her to the courthouse. Then, we will go to the church for Pastor Green's signature on the marriage license."

"That's fine, Mike," I am so very fond of this newest member of our family. "I'll call you if we need you."

"OK," he replies. "I'll be back in an hour or less." He quietly walks through the kitchen and out the back door. I listen for the sound of his truck as he drives away.

“You're exhausted,” Dan says, looking at me softly.

“Yes,” I whisper. “perhaps more than exhausted. I can't describe the weariness.”

“Do you want to go upstairs to lie down? I will come get you if Liz's condition changes,” he offers.

“I can't leave," I say, "I only have this time, these minutes with her. I'll sleep later. You can go upstairs if you'd like, though.”

“No,” he says, stretching. “I'm not willing to give up my minutes with her either.” He pulls me to him again. I rest against him and find comfort in his steady heartbeat.

“Who do you love more?” I ask against his shirt. “Me or Liz?”

“Neither,” he says, gently. “Or maybe I should say 'both.' I love you both more than I ever thought possible. I just love you each very differently.”

I marvel that for twenty-seven years I have shared my man with my best friend. He has never come between us and we have never fought over him. He has never given us a need. He is that kind of man who can love completely, simultaneously, and entirely differently. Another incredible gift.

~*~

Guatemala changed me. Actually, that initial trip changed all of us. Spending seven days serving people in the rugged mountains reshaped my view of my needs and my wants. I wanted much, I needed little.

I changed much. Liz changed more. She had already lived her life being generous and giving much. She lived far below her means, learning long ago that it was always much better to give than to receive. I think she considered herself a generous person before Guatemala. After that trip, though, she became a magnanimous benefactress. I was given a front-row seat to watch her generosity expound. She was a gift in action.

"Do these children have an opportunity for education?" Liz asked our translator, while Dan examined a young boy.

"Not often," the translator responded. "Some parents find a way to get their children to the cities to be able to go to school. However, most of the people here are poor farmers who do not have the means to send their children to the schools in the city."

"How often do these people receive medical care?" she asked.

"This clinic is open five days a week. However, we only have doctors when they come from America to help us," Juan, the translator, stated.

"How often is that," Liz continued, peppering Juan with questions while she held young, Javier.

Javier sat still while Dan looked at the infection on his leg.

"It depends," Juan answered gently. "Some years, lots of doctors come and the clinic is very busy. Other years, though, maybe only one or two doctors come and the people have to wait."

"What does the clinic offer when there are no doctors?" Liz asked, over Javier's crying.

"We do what we can with the supplies the doctors leave for us," Juan responded. "And, we pray to God for help. You are God's answer to our prayers. We find that the more we pray, the more doctors come to help."

"Oh," Liz stammered. "Dr. Dan is the answer to your prayers. I am just here to know how to pray."

"You help too," Juan insisted, looking at Liz's arms. Javier has stopped crying and has snuggled into Liz's comforting arms.

Later, after a filling dinner of black beans, tortillas, fruit, and limeade back at the hotel, I found Liz sitting quietly on the deck of her hotel room. Silent tears streamed down her cheeks as she sat with her eyes closed and her hand on her Bible.

"What is it, Liz?" I asked quietly, not sure if I wanted to interrupt. I was confident, though, that I couldn't walk away.

"This," she whispered. "All of this. The need is incredible. It is overwhelming to me. It's just so much."

"I understand," I said, looking off into the mountains. "That

is why we are here."

"No!" she answered, emphatically. "Being here is not enough. The need is much greater than that. I want to do more."

"Like what?" I asked.

"I don't know yet," she mumbled. "I'm praying for an answer. Pray with me?"

"I'd love to," I smiled.

Right there on the hotel room deck, in the waning sunlight, we knelt and prayed. We specifically asked God to show us how to do more. Neither of us, though, had any idea the ways in which He would answer our prayers.

When we opened our eyes, He took our breath away. The evening blue sky was painted with huge brush strokes of reds and yellows mixed with oranges and pinks. We both watched in rapture at God's creativity as He lowered the fireball sun in the Western sky. We wept with thanksgiving to serve such an awesome Creator. It was the most brilliant sunset I had ever witnessed. It was a rare gift that neither of us has forgotten.

Returning to the States was difficult for Liz. She returned simply for Jenny and Mark. Had they not been in high school and college, I think she would have simply stayed in the Guatemalan mountains, loving on the people there.

A few weeks after we returned, Liz ran across the cul-de-sac and into my house. I was working on an art project for Dan. It was a drawing of a snapshot I had taken in Guatemala of Dan holding a small girl who had a severe hernia. Dan scheduled the child for surgery with a surgical team that arrived after we left. After the operation was scheduled, he spent some time playing with the young Mariana. By the end of her visit, she had him wrapped around her little finger.

"Whoa!" Liz said, as she barged up to the table before coming to a complete stop. "That is incredible!"

"You like it?" I asked. I continued, erasing and reworking Mariana's hand.

"It's incredible," she repeated. "Is it Dan's birthday gift?"

"Yes," I said. "I thought maybe he'd like to hang it in his office."

"I think you should consider hanging it at my house," she quipped.

"But, it's not your birthday," I answered, still trying to get Mariana's hand just right.

"No," she said. "But, I'd take good care of it!"

"I'm sure you would," I answered. "What are you doing here anyway?"

"Oh, yeah," she remembered. "I wanted to run an idea past you and Dan and get your opinion."

"OK," I said, completely distracted by my artwork. "Do you want to talk now or after dinner?"

"After dinner," she announced. "I'm waiting for a phone call and I want to talk to you and Dan together. How does Chinese t take-out sound tonight?"

"Great!" I gratefully replied. I loved the nights I didn't have to cook. "When?"

"I'll call for carry-out. Do you think Dan would be willing to pick it up?"

"Probably," I responded. "You'll want to call him anyway. I'm not sure what he would want to order."

"OK," she said, walking toward the door. "I'll take care of it. Any chance, you'll let me see the finished project before you wrap it up for his birthday next week?"

"Probably," I mumbled. "Just remind me."

"Don't worry," she replied, before shutting the door, "I will!"

"There it is," I muttered to myself, finishing Mariana's hand. "I finally got it right."

An hour later, I placed the finished piece in the portfolio in the back of my closet and ordered the matte and frame. I loved the feeling of a project well done. Even more, I loved giving Dan gifts I knew he'd love. I got it all put away before dinner time at Liz's.

"I can't get Javier and Guatemala out of my mind," Liz stated

after we had eaten our fill. "The night we prayed and witnessed that brilliant sunset I knew God was calling me to do something, I just didn't know what. I've prayed and fasted since we returned and I am confident that God is leading me to give to ministry in Guatemala like I've never given before."

Dan and I listened quietly. I could not fathom how Liz, who was the most generous person I knew, could give like she's never given before. We said nothing and Liz continued.

"When Mom and Dad passed away, they left the Estate in a trust for Mark and Jenny. I was given full use of it and provision for upkeep. The stipulation is that only Mark and Jenny can sell it. The rest of their personal financial estate was left to me. I retained their attorney to help me liquidate their assets. Believe me when I tell you, I had no idea the amount of assets my father had accumulated. When I add that amount to the trust I inherited from my grandparents, the amount is quite a bit of money."

Dan laughed out loud. "It must be something for you to admit that it is quite a bit of money."

"Well," she said laughing with him. "It's enough that I would like to start a mission agency based at the Estate. Jenny is a junior in high school. In two years, I would like to sell this house and live exclusively in New York. For now, though, I am working with my own attorney to start a not-for-profit agency that will serve to

provide education, medicine, food, and clothing to the mountainous peoples of Guatemala."

"Wow," I said. "That is great! Aren't there already agencies in place though?"

"Yes," Liz responded. "There are some highly qualified agencies that serve Guatemala. Every agency I contacted though, reminded me that the need is great. I would like to partner with a couple of different agencies. Maybe together we can do more than one agency could do alone."

"You've put a lot of thought into this," Dan commented.

"You have no idea," Liz replied. "How would you like to give up your practice here to be the physician of record for this agency and to travel to Guatemala several times a year? The organization would pay you a stipend."

Dan smiled. "You aren't the only one who has been doing a lot of thinking since we've gotten back. I would love to do something like that. I really appreciate that you are thinking ahead. Two years gives me time to transition my patients to another practitioner in our office."

"I'd like to help," I said, after a few minutes. "I'm just not sure what I can do right now since Ryan has several years of school left."

"I was hoping you would say that," Liz smiled at me. "I can't

imagine doing this without both of you! Kris, I was hoping you would help me come up with a name for our organization and a logo."

"Hey," I stated, enthusiastically, "that I can do."

Liz brewed coffee while Dan did the dishes and I put away our leftovers. We three friends spent the rest of the night praying and dreaming big dreams for Javier, Mariana, and the countless children we had seen. God used those children to change us. We counted them as gifts.

chapter 26

"The birth of Solo Dios Basta Ministries, or Dios Basta, as Liz calls it," Jana murmurs. "I have spoken with Liz about this ministry often. I just never asked her what the name means."

"Solo Dios Basta means "God alone suffices" in Spanish. We wanted a name that the Guatemalan people would understand and a name that would give glory only to God and not to ourselves," Dan replies, quietly. "It is His ministry and we will continue it for as long as He wills it."

My heart catches again. It is hard to swallow. How will we continue without her? How will we serve without the one who served the most? How will we go on without the one who dared to dream the dream?

My throat burns hot and tears spill over. I look at my ailing friend whose body is struggling for each breath. I realize that, though she is here with us physically, she has already gone. Her body continues to fight and struggle to function as it was created to do. There is, however, nothing left of the friend I met twenty-eight years ago. I weep.

Dan continues the story for me, as Jana and Becki listen. I can no longer form words around the lump that threatens to suffocate me. Instead, I climb in the queen bed and lay close, hoping to impart some life into her, and knowing that I am neither the giver nor the taker of life. My tears soak her pillow.

~*~

Liz never dreamed a dream that she didn't do her best to fulfill. The development of Solo Dios Basta Ministries was no exception. She found renewed purpose and poured her life into it. Liz was tireless and creative in fundraising. She hosted black-tie dinners at the Estate, recorded her own CDs of harp and piano music, and convinced people in the music world to donate and to bid at silent auctions. More than anything, she raised the bar on sacrificial giving. She gave of herself, her time, and her money radically and without complaint. She sold most of her possessions to fund the ministry. Eventually, she sold her house, her harp, and her piano to run the ministry full time from the Estate. She even sold her sedan. She chose, instead, to drive Ash's old pick-up truck.

Liz changed completely. Things like a leather interior vehicle no longer mattered to her. Instead, she saw everything through the lens of people's needs. If she owned something that could be sold to provide education or clothing for someone else, she would often sell that very item. She spoke to groups and organizations about the difference between wants and needs. Though never really one to flaunt her wealth, people noticed the radical change in Liz. It gave credence to her words when she spoke. She modeled love in action.

Though she completely fell in love with Guatemala and the Guatemalan people, she only ever traveled there once. She firmly believed that the money she would spend to travel back and forth could be put to better use by sending doctors, nurses, dentists, and surgeons. She converted Ash's office at the Estate to the headquarters for Solo Dios Basta Ministries and from there she would send medical teams and mission teams to heal the sick, build schools and clinics, and to educate. She said she never tired of traveling to Guatemala from her office chair.

With Mark living in California, Jenny moved to the Estate with Liz. She had finished her cosmetology degree while still in high school, earning dual credit. Once she moved to New York, she became licensed and found a job in a local salon. She also took Spanish classes at the local community college to further the few Spanish speaking skills she learned in high school. Jenny fully expected to live in Guatemala and help run the school there. Sometimes, though, God's ways are higher than ours, even when we do not understand.

Within six months, both houses in the cul-de-sac sold. We followed Liz to the Estate. Liz gave us our original honeymoon suite, the guest house, and Kris, Ryan, and I moved in. A local physician had opened an indigent clinic near Buffalo and offered me a job. Though it was a fifty minute drive to the clinic, the work was perfect. I felt as if I were finally doing what it was God had created me to do... helping those in need. After working together for a year, Dr. Joe Wysong and I became partners. We both support Solo Dios Basta Ministries. Twice a year, we closed the clinic and took our staff members, those who were willing to come with us, to the clinic in Guatemala. These trips have become amazing times of seeing God at work. Many of our staff members have come to know Jesus through the testimony of the Guatemalan believers.

Ryan willingly transitioned to a new state and a new community for the rest of his school years. Though he was the most difficult child as a baby, he certainly was the easiest one to raise. Ryan was thrilled with the football program at his new school, and half-way through his sophomore year, he found himself as starting center for the varsity football team. Later, that position earned him a football scholarship for college.

Often, God's blessings come after our obedience. We have seen His blessings all over our lives these few years that we've lived here at the Estate. He has blessed the ministry abundantly. He has also blessed us individually beyond our wildest imagination. I don't think we truly realized the blessings until we started counting the gifts. It was Liz, of course, who influenced Kris and I to count gifts.

"Kris," Liz called one evening from the "big house" as we called it. "Is Dan available?" Kris handed me the phone without even answering Liz's question.

"Hey Lizzie," I said.

"Dan, I think you need to take me to the hospital," she said, shakily. "I just coughed up some blood."

I had treated Liz for chronic bronchitis over the winter. She would seemingly get better for a little while, but she never seemed to get well. We had tried several different antibiotics to get rid of the infection. It was as if her body just couldn't fight it off.

"Meet me by my truck," I said, grabbing my coat and boots. "I'll be right there."

"What?" Kris asked me.

"I'm taking Liz into Buffalo. She needs an MRI," I replied, forcing my voice to be calm.

"Let's go," my girl answered, grabbing her own coat and boots.

We three, who have traveled so much of life together, piled into my SUV with four-wheel drive and fairly flew over the snow covered country roads to get to the hospital. My clinical brain tried to tell my emotional heart that there was no immediate rush to get there. In response, my sensitive heart essentially told my professional brain to shut up and keep driving. I tried to maintain an image of the calm, cool, and collected medical professional. I failed miserably.

"Dan?" Liz asked, as I took a turn at thirty miles an hour. "Am I dying or are you going to kill me in route to the hospital?" Humor was still Liz's greatest weapon in times of stress.

I had learned long ago to be one hundred percent honest and upfront with this amazing woman sitting in the front seat next to me. For whatever reason, she had an uncanny ability to see right through me. If you were to ask me who knew me better, Kris or Liz, I'm not sure what my answer would be. I would probably tell you that it would depend on the circumstances. In this circumstance, I knew that she knew that I was scared to death.

"It's potentially serious, Liz," I said carefully. "I don't know why I didn't think of this before. I'm sorry. I should have thought of this. I could have known. The reason you can't seem to kick

this bronchitis is that the cancer could be back. I should have done blood work or ordered an MRI or something before now. I'm so sorry, Lizzie."

In my honesty, I revealed the struggle in my heart. I was scared. I was mad at myself and I was ashamed. As her physician, I should have seen this coming. I could have caught it before. I failed the one I loved.

"Dan," she said, softly and slowly, "this changes nothing. God knows and He knew. If you take the blame for this, then you are essentially saying that you are like God. I love you. Now, get over yourself. You are no good to me if you are wrapped up in self-loathing. I need you to be my ears and listen for me tonight. Then I will need you to explain all that was said to me in the simplest terms possible." Just like that, Liz simultaneously loved on me and put me in my place. According to her, I had a job to do.

Practicing medicine definitely has its perks. One, of which, is the professional courtesy that I receive any time I am a patient or am with a patient. Pulling into the parking lot with Liz was no different. Later, she commented on having the red carpet rolled out for her. At registration and at each department she was sent to, she had very little wait time, including the wait to have the MRI read by the radiologist. Looking back, I count it all as gifts.

"Dan," Dr. Leigh Chen said, as she saw me in the hallway,

"may I speak to you first?" I knew she was coming to discuss Liz's MRI results.

"Sure," I said confidently, hiding the fear deep within. I was professionally curious and personally apprehensive all at the same time.

"Let's step in here," she said, pointing to an empty conference room.

I had met Leigh Chen a few times at various charitable events for the medical community. She was incredibly intelligent and renowned in the oncology realm. I was grateful that Dr. Chen was the oncologist on call that evening. Later, I would be even more grateful when she agreed to see Liz in her practice.

"I have read her history," she started, looking at Liz's chart. "She's fought this breast cancer valiantly. As you well know, there is much about cancer we don't understand. We don't know why it can seemingly go away and then reappear years later. We don't know what triggers it to awaken again. The one thing I do know, though, is that Liz's cancer is back, with a vengeance. Look at this," she handed me Liz's MRI.

In that moment, I knew I was over my head medically. The images caused me to stop breathing for a moment. Both of Liz's lungs showed multiple lesions. In my vague understanding of oncology, I knew this was bad.

"I consulted with a few colleagues here. We all agree. This is stage 4 lung cancer and it is aggressive. We feel that it should be treated as such."

I stared at the MRI images. The lines between my personal life and my professional life blurred, as did the images I was holding. Tears pooled, and I quietly handed Dr. Chen the images. I said nothing. Instead, I stood and walked back to the waiting room where Liz and Kris sat. I knew Dr. Chen was right behind me.

"I've got to fight this," Liz said on the way home. "There is so much to do. I want to continue the work at Dios Basta. I want to fight this disease more now than I ever did when the kids were little."

In a moment that was God ordained, we three talked all the way home. We talked about fighting this round of cancer and what it entailed. We spoke of Dr. Chen's advice of aggressive therapy. We discussed the ravage effects of undergoing chemo and radiation simultaneously. We communicated about the ministry and where each of us saw it going.

The fifty minute drive home did not give us enough time to say all we needed to say. The conversation spilled over into the living room of the big house. With hot coffee and a crackling fire, we talked until the wee hours of the morning.

A fireside chat... time slowed just for us... a generous gift.

chapter 27

Empty of tears, I stay by Liz. I am fully aware that my presence changes nothing for her. Instead, it changes everything for me. Lying together in her bed... Liz tucked in under the electric blanket and me on top of it... I begin the process of releasing my friend. Up until now, I had held on tightly, white knuckled, refusing to let go. Lying side by side with Liz laboring for each breath, convinces me I must let go.

Liz stirs next to me. I'm not sure if she is uncomfortable because I am next to her, or if she is uncomfortable because the end is near. I don't know if I should move or if I should stay. I don't know what to do... what to say.

Becki gently nudges me. “Kris, I can give her more morphine. I just need you to move for me.”

“Gladly,” I mumble. I feel so discombobulated. I am weary

beyond comprehension. I've worn the same clothing for twenty-three hours. I cannot even remember the last time I bathed. I need to brush my teeth. I need a shower. I need clean clothes. Here I am again, confusing need with want. In my befuddled mind, I know that I want clean clothes and I need my friend. I want one more lucid moment with her. One more joke, one more laugh. The whisper in my soul, though, convinces me that one more will never be enough. I gently slide off of Liz's bed.

"I'm going over to take a shower, brush my teeth, and change my clothes," I mumble to Dan, Jana, and Becki. I have just grieved uproariously in front of them. I find it difficult to look any of them in the eye.

"Are you sure you want to leave?" Dan reaches for me as I walk through the kitchen to the back door.

"I need a few minutes," I say slowly. "I won't be long."

"OK," he says, looking deep into my eyes. "It's okay to grieve, you know."

I say nothing. What is there to say? I turn and walk out the door, quietly shutting it behind me. The rain that started the day before continues. A steady rain drenches the soaked earth forming puddles everywhere. It seems that I step in every single one on the short walk to our house. My shoes are saturated, my socks are soaked, and my feet are wet. I hardly notice. I feel incredibly numb and yet my heart hurts much. How does that work?

A quick hot shower does nothing to warm my heart or ease my pain. I am, however, clean with fresh breath and fresh clothing when I run back to the big house. I do my best to avoid the major mud puddles on the return trip.

Shaking off the biggest rain drops, the first thing I notice is the smell of fresh coffee. I see Mark in the kitchen. He's freshly clean, too. As I walk through, he hands me a hot cup of coffee, with lots of vanilla creamer, just the way I like it.

"How is she?" I ask, suddenly in a hurry to get back to Liz's side.

"Same," Becki says, softly. "You look like you feel a little better."

"Not sure I feel any better," I answer. "Just have fresh breath now."

Somehow in that little bit of small talk, I feel comfortable with Becki again. In her line of work, she sees people handle grief in all kinds of different ways. Becki is comfortable with grief. I am the one who is not.

"Do you feel like taking the story over again?" Dan gently asks me. "Or, do you want me to continue?"

"Have you told any more?" I ask, sitting down on the edge of the bed.

"No," he says, "it's been quiet in here. If you don't mind, I'm going to run home and shower quickly while you tell about the book."

"OK," I smile, weakly. "Be careful of the mud puddles."

~*~

Liz agreed to Dr. Chen's aggressive treatment plan. After Liz had a port inserted for chemotherapy, Dr. Chen ordered the chemotherapy and radiation to be done simultaneously. Five days a week, we were scheduled to drive to Buffalo for treatments and appointments. Thankfully, Jenny quit her job at the salon and took over the office work for the ministry. Liz relaxed a bit knowing that Dios Basta was in such good hands.

On the way into Buffalo for Liz's first chemo treatment, we stopped for lunch and a little window shopping. After soup and sandwiches, we stepped into a little bookstore and wandered around. Liz found an interesting book. She said it would keep her company during the long days of low white cell counts. She began reading it that afternoon.

While I flipped through the waiting room's selection of outdated magazines, Liz sat next to me, mesmerized. Silently, she turned the pages. Without a sound, tears fell.

"Are you okay?" I asked quietly.

"It's this book, it moves me," she said slowly, closing the book and wiping her eyes. "Do you remember how moved we were at

the sunset in Guatemala?"

"I hope I never forget!" I exclaimed. "It was the most beautiful thing I have ever seen."

"This book," she says, patting the cover. "This book moves me in that same way. I feel as if I am moved beyond myself. In reading these words, I know God is already at work changing me."

Liz was a ferocious reader. She had the entire work finished by the next day. She handed it to me on the way to Buffalo.

"I want you to read this," she said.

"Don't you want to finish it first?" I asked.

"I did," she answered. "I read it last night. I want to read it again and again and again. I just want you to read it first."

"Is it really that good?" I wondered.

"Yes," she said firmly. "And more. It is more than that good. I'd like to stop at that bookstore and buy another copy. As soon as you read it, we can discuss it."

"Yes ma'am," I teased. "But, don't expect me to read it all in one day."

"You will," she smiled. "Well, maybe not all in one day, but you won't be able to put it down."

"You're sure about that?" I chuckled. "What if I don't like it."

"You'll like it," she said, watching out her window. "Honestly, it's that good."

Over the years, Liz had given me many books to read. I only ever finished a few of them. The rest of them just became dust collectors on my bookshelf. I just don't possess Liz's appetite to read. With this book, though, it was different. She was right... of course. Not only did I finish it, I read it in just a couple of days.

Reading the book began a new work in both of us. The author challenged us to live a life of gratitude, finding things to thank God for. It was in the reading of this book that we began to count our gifts... those little everyday things, that when seen through the eyes of gratitude, become special things.

It probably goes without saying that Liz was much more bold in counting gifts and being grateful than I was. We both decided to keep a notebook and write down our gratitude lists. Liz, however, would tell people how thankful she was for them. Before long, she became a bit of a celebrity at the cancer center.

"Are you comfortable?" asked a nurse one day after getting Liz's chemotherapy started.

"Yes, I am," Liz commented. "Thank you for your great care of me. You are a gift."

I couldn't tell you how many times Liz called her care givers "gifts." Every single time she did, they would walk away from her presence standing a little straighter and smiling a little more. By counting gifts, Liz became a gift to others. Her attitude of gratitude and her compliments to the staff became legendary. Soon hospital employees sought her out.

"I'm just here to... ah... um...," a young hospital volunteer stated, coming into Liz's curtained area. "Um, to empty the trash. Yes, I will just empty your trash."

"Thank you, Sweetheart," Liz said, sincerely. "I appreciate your care for me as I sit here waiting for the chemo to finish. Thanks for taking care of my trash. You are a gift to me." Had I not seen it with my own eyes, I'm not sure I would have believed it. That young girl was practically giddy as she left Liz's area.

"Isn't it amazing the difference gratitude makes?" Liz spoke quietly. "I wasted too many years assuming things would just get done. For instance, I always assumed someone would eventually empty the trash can. I never thought to thank the people that are serving me in such a lowly capacity."

"I'm not sure she was actually serving in such a lowly capacity," I chuckled. "I think she just wanted to hear you call her a gift."

"Maybe," Liz thought for a minute. "But, it doesn't matter. Truly, she is a gift."

Early spring turned into full-fledged warm days and budding trees. Flowers bloomed, birds sang, and the tree frogs peeped long into the night. Though she was very sick from the extreme treatments, Liz never failed to mention how thankful she was for the new green leaves and the smell of the lilac blossoms.

Each trip to Buffalo became harder for her. I began to dread the trip, including the time there and the journey home. This was, by far, the sickest I had ever seen my friend. It pained me to watch her. It hurt me more to know that our trips were not making a difference with the cancer.

"Hello, Liz," Dr. Chen said, poking her head through the curtain partition. "How are you today?"

"I'm good, Dr. Chen," Liz said, slowly. The sores in her mouth made speaking, eating, and drinking very difficult.

"She's lying," I told Dr. Chen. "Her mouth hurts so much she can hardly speak."

"I'm sorry, Liz," Dr. Chen started, "and you too, Kris. Those mouth sores are extremely painful and I hate that you have to experience them."

"It's okay," Liz said. "Really."

"Thank you for understanding," Dr. Chen replied, pulling over a chair from the cubicle next to us. "Do you mind if I sit for a while?" Dr. Leigh Chen kept a very busy schedule. I knew that she typically didn't take time to sit down with her patients. Her presence made me leery.

"Liz," she began. "We got your blood work back. I will be

honest, we are not getting the results we had hoped to get with this aggressive treatment."

"Dr. Leigh," Liz replied. "I am so grateful to you and to your team. Please, don't feel like you can't ever be honest with me. I need your honesty as much as I need your professional care."

"Ok," Dr. Leigh Chen paused for a moment, and then continued, "I've conferred with some of the best oncologists in the nation this morning. We unanimously agree that your cancer is not responding to this particular form of chemotherapy. We do not know why." For a moment no one said anything. Liz and I were trying to comprehend all that Dr. Chen was saying in her few words. She continued, "We also do not know what else to do."

"Well," Liz smiled, "I know what to do. I will continue to be grateful and continue to pray. I will count my gifts for as many days as God gives me. Today, I am counting you, Dr. Leigh, as a gift to me. I am blessed to be under your care. Thank you for taking care of me."

"I think I'm the one blessed," Leigh Chen said, wiping her eyes. "You have blessed many throughout this facility, Liz."

"What's next, Dr. Chen?" I tentatively asked.

"We will finish this round of chemo today," she said. "Kris, I want you to take Liz home and let her rest. We will give her body a week of rest and then reevaluate next week In the meantime, I

will continue to research and seek advice as to how to treat this."

"Thank you, Dr. Leigh," Liz extended her hand. "Thank you for your personal interest in caring for me."

"Trust me when I say that it has been my pleasure!" Leigh Chen reached down and hugged Liz instead of taking her hand. "Thank you for the ways that you bless all of us."

I saw Dr. Leigh Chen wipe her eyes again as she slipped out around the curtain and I knew my eyes were leaking too.

"We just keep saying 'thank you,' Kris," Liz gently stated, looking at me. "We still count gifts."

Later, I sat next to Dan and cried as I recounted the day. I told him all that Dr. Chen had told us. I gave him the copy of Liz's blood work that the nurse sent home with us. I listened as he called Leigh Chen at home and conferred with her. And, when he hung up quietly, I sobbed. I had heard enough.

"How do we live a life of gratitude while she dies?" I asked, blubbering. "How do you count sickness and cancer and death as gifts anyway?"

"We watch Liz and we learn," he said, holding me. "She's teaching us."

"You know," I slobbered. "She's always on my gratitude list each day."

"Mine, too," he whispered. "Mine, too."

chapter 28

“Was that her last chemo treatment?” Becki asks.

“Yes,” I answer. “She had her last treatment at the end of May. Dr. Chen ordered an MRI the very next week and showed Liz the results. Liz chose to live her last days, how ever many she had, without mouth sores, nausea, and vomiting.”

“Did she continue with the radiation?” Becki probes.

“No,” I smile, weakly. “She decided she was done traveling to Buffalo every single day. She wanted to be here, at the Estate. In fact, she hasn't left. Two weeks after that chemo, she kicked Jenny out of the Dios Basta office and resumed working for the ministry.”

“She hasn't left,” Becki questions, “at all?”

“Well,” I chuckle, “all summer long she only left the Estate for church. She often commented that this place, this home, is exactly where she wanted to be."

"So, you were the one to do the grocery shopping and other errands?"

"Yes," I respond, "and I did it gladly. Liz once thanked me for the gift of giving her that time here. She spent the summer walking the old trails through the woods, puttering around in the yard, and sitting in the gazebo."

"When was she hospitalized this fall?" Becki asks quietly.

"She wasn't," I reply. "When she knew the end was near, she called your office and made her own appointment. Dr. Leigh Chen faxed the orders and Liz was able to stay here."

"Has her doctor seen her?" Though she is asking many questions, I comprehend the nature of Becki's query. Becki serves many patients through her job as a Hospice nurse. I am beginning to realize Liz's conditions are most unique. I doubt Becki has ever served a patient like Liz.

"Yes," I answer. "Dr. Chen has been here several times to visit with Liz. Per Liz's request, though, Dr. Chen gave Liz's care over to Dan ten days ago when Hospice first came. Dan is again Liz's primary care physician. Leigh Chen calls him regularly to get updates."

"What do I do?" Dan asks, walking back into Liz's room. I now understand why Becki thought I felt better after my shower. Clean clothes, fresh breath, and a shower dramatically improve one's appearance. Dan looks great.

"You care for Liz," I say, appreciatively.

"For as long as I can," he softly says, sitting on the other side of Liz's bed. He gently reaches out and feels for her pulse.

"Kris," he whispers. "I think you should call Mike and Jenny and find the boys. It won't be long."

How? How do I call Jenny and casually mention that she should hurry, but, that she might not make it? I find Luke and Mark and tell them that Dan's calling us all together again.

"Hi Mom," I turn to that voice. The one I have known for nineteen years. "I couldn't stay away. I brought Grandma too."

"Hi, dear," my mom says. "I couldn't stay away, either. I called Ryan and asked him to pick me up." Together, I envelop them into a group hug. I need them. I need all of us together.

"For once," I say to Ryan through my tears, "I am so glad you didn't listen to your mother and stay at school."

"I need to be here, Mom," he says, towering over me. "I need you and Dad. I need to be with Aunt Lizzie."

"Well, come on in then," I reply. "I'm trying to find Mark and

Luke. I need to call Mike and Jenny too."

"I'll find Mark and Luke," Ryan says, turning for the stairway.

"I'll call Jenny," Mom says, reaching for the kitchen phone.

In this moment, I realize how grateful I am for these people... these gifts... who I desperately need and who need me. This ongoing need to love and be loved is fulfilled with these I love the most.

These gifts that Liz insisted be with her until the end are my gifts too.

~*~

The summer was gorgeous. Warm luscious days filled with brilliant sunshine. Though her MRI showed cancer everywhere, Liz felt great. She would spend the cool mornings walking through the woods or wandering around the yard. Somedays she would tend to the flowers. Other days she would simply sit in the shade of the gazebo and watch the pond.

"What are you doing?" I asked one day, finding her on the porch.

"Soaking it all in," she said. "I feel as if each of these days has been a special gift just for me. You heard Dr. Chen say that,

based on my MRI, I shouldn't feel this good, but now that I am over the effects of the chemo, I feel great. These days are gifts, Kris. Gifts just for me. I want to stop and savor them."

"Kind of like eating your dessert slowly, huh?" I said, handing her a bowl of ice cream.

"Mmm.... thank you," she replied with a smile. "Yes, I am savoring every day slowly and tasting each moment."

For three months, Liz lived and played. She worked on the ministry and worshipped in church on Sunday. Her gratitude list grew by leaps and bounds. I could hardly keep up and eventually gave up. Liz counted enough for both of us. Thankfully, she often counted out loud. Her list became mine.

"Did you see the moon tonight?" Liz asked, one early September night. "It's big, fat, and so bright. I had to put it on my list."

"I'll put it on mine too," I said, walking to the door to go home for the night.

"Kris!" she said sharply.

"What?" I asked

"You cheat!" she accused. "You can't count my things as yours. You've got to find your own gifts and make your own list."

"Really?" I teased. "Does it say that in the Counting Gifts

Rulebook?"

"No," she huffed. "It says that in my rulebook. Get your own gifts!" I laughed and shut the door behind me.

For days, though, Liz was bothered. "You really need to find your own gifts, Kris," she said to me in the kitchen one afternoon.

"It's okay, Liz," I replied handing her a cup of tea. "I'm only giving you a hard time. I do have things on my list that are not on yours."

"Like what?" she asked.

"Well, if you promise not to copy, I'll tell you," I gently mocked. "You, Elizabeth Renee Ashley-Bower, are on my list every single day and I doubt you are on your own list. So, see, I list something you don't."

"You so cheat," she sighed. "You can't list something more than once."

"Would you kindly stop making up the rules?" I laughed.

"Yes, if you will let me make up the rules one more time," she quietly stated.

"What?" I asked. I suddenly realized that we were no longer joking.

"I want to tell you how I am leaving my estate, this Estate," she started. "I spent the morning on the phone with my attorney.

My updated will and advanced directive are all written out. I faxed his office a copy with my signature. He has it on record and has been retained to see that my will is carried out."

"Liz, no, please," I begged. I wasn't ready to discuss Liz's death and her advanced directive. I wanted to stay in the warmth of this summer forever. Just as I had failed to notice the leaves changing colors on the trees, I had also failed to notice the deep fatigue changing the face of my friend. She was loosing her luster.

"Kris, we have lived twenty-eight years together," she began, ignoring my plea. "I need you now more than ever. Please, do this for me."

"Now?" I asked, trying to calm my restless heart.

"Yes, please," she said, forcing a smile. "I'd like to talk to you about this now. I'd like the peace of knowing that all is taken care of. Here's a notebook and a pen, I think you may need them."

The next two hours were spent with me filling the notebook with Liz's directions. We talked about her last days and how she absolutely insisted to be allowed to live her last days here at the Estate. There would be no more days in the hospital for her.

"I don't need a hospital. Hospitals save people and I will be beyond saving. I don't need doctors. I have Dan," she said. "And, I've already spoken to him about this. He and Dr. Chen will get

me an appointment with Hospice. He's even agreed to go with me, if his schedule will allow. He agrees that there is no reason why I cannot live out my life right here at the Estate."

"OK, then," I sighed. This talk of death and last wishes... this discussion of comfort measures and Hospice... all of this was more than I wanted to deal with. I only listened and filled the notebook because I loved her. I wanted to be the one she could rely on. I truly wanted to do all that and more for my lifelong friend. Only, I didn't know how.

"I'd like you to be sure everyone is here when my time comes," she continued. "I know Ryan and Mark may not be able to be here exactly when I go and I understand. I just would like to be surrounded by my family, my gifts, until the end."

"I will do my best," I said, making a note of it. I didn't need to write a note to remind myself to gather everyone at the appropriate time. I wrote because I needed something to do in that moment. Something to keep my restless heart firmly planted in that kitchen chair.

The list in my notebook expanded. Page after page of written instructions from Liz. She wanted to talk about Jenny's wedding in May and had visions to implement for Dios Basta. She had thoughts for the use of the Estate and for the clinic that Dan and Joe ran. It seemed as if she had ideas for everything. I now fully understood how she used her time at night. While plagued with insomnia, she dreamed big dreams.

"Of course, there is the will and how everything is bequeathed," she proceeded. "I've designated you to be the executor of my estate. Not this Estate, that belongs to my kids, but my personal estate..."

"Whoa!" I said, interrupting her. "You want me to do what?"

"Did I not already ask you to be the executor?" she asked.

"Ah, no!" I stammered. "Listen, I love you. You know that. I can take notes right now for you. I can gather family. I can make sure that Jenny is married off in a beautiful ceremony and I can even make sure she gets down the aisle. I cannot, however, be the one who says, 'you get this' and 'you get that.' I can't do it, Liz. Please, ask Mark or Dan."

"Well, Mark isn't here and I am honestly not sure how he would handle knowing my financial information, I've already asked Dan to help me medically," she informed. "Honestly, I thought I had already asked you. I'm sorry that this came as a surprise. Really, Kris, I need you to help me with this. I promise this will be the last thing I ask of you."

"Not funny," I huffed at her poor attempt at a joke.

"I thought it was," she smiled.

"It's just that this is too much. I feel overwhelmed. I want you to be here forever with Dan and me. I want to sit by the pond on lazy summer evenings with you. I want to talk by the fireplace on cold winter's nights with you. I want to dream big dreams with you. I want to laugh and cry. I want to live and count gifts with you, forever," I choked back the sob that was surfacing. "I don't want to lose you!"

Liz held me while I sobbed. In the deep recesses of my mind, I realized the irony of it all. I should have been holding Liz. I should have been the strong one. Instead, in her last good days, Liz was strong and I was weak.

"Throw a party," she said to lighten the mood.

"What?" I slobbered.

"A party. Throw a party when I die," she smiled at me. "Please I don't want a drab funeral where everyone is all decked out in black. DO NOT WEAR BLACK! It honestly doesn't look good on you. Wear something bright and cheery. Maybe even bring balloons. I've already ordered my memorial stone and Pastor Jon Green has agreed to officiate the graveside memorial service for my family. I don't want a big service and I don't want a

big deal made over me. Please don't be sad for me. I will be dancing in heaven waiting for all of you."

And, just like that, she gave her final wishes concerning her funeral. Simple wishes that completely overwhelmed me. The tears continued.

"More than anything," she said, gently brushing tears from my face, "continue counting. Count with me to the end and keep counting after I've gone."

chapter 29

Jenny and Mike rush in. They drop wet coats, boots, and umbrellas on the floor in the laundry room by the back door and hurry to Liz's bedside.

"Is it too late?" Jenny asks, out of breath.

"No," Dan whispers, "she's still with us... for a little while."

Mike reaches over to shake Ryan's hand and Jenny gives Grandma Murphy a hug and a kiss on the cheek.

"I heard congratulations are in order," Mom whispers to Jenny.

"Yes," she smiles back. "We just went to the courthouse to make it official."

"Are you still going to have a ceremony in May?" Grandma Murphy asks.

"No," Jenny continues. "We decided this morning to cancel all the plans. I'll lose the deposit on the reception facility. I had not yet ordered the invitations, cake, or flowers, so we won't lose any money there. Mom designed my dress. We were still looking for a dressmaker to make it, so we are not out any money there either. Mike and I would rather use the money we would spend on the wedding for Solo Dios Basta. We want to go to Guatemala and touch base with the locals in the school and clinic and see what more we can do to help."

"I'm sure your mama is proud of you," Grandma Murphy hugs Jenny again.

"I hope so," Jenny sighs.

While we gather and talk, Dan continues to monitor Liz. His fingers rest against her carotid artery. He is constantly counting her pulse and her respirations.

"Lizzie," he gently begins. "We are all here. Ryan picked up Mom Murphy this morning and they are here with us. We are all gathered around you. Kris is sitting on your right side with Ryan, Mark, and Luke. Jenny, Mike, and Mom are with me on your left. Jana and Becki are here as well. We love you Lizzie. We will stay here for as long as you need us."

Mark steps forward and reaches for Liz's hand. He continues what Dan started, "Mom, it's me, Mark. I'm holding your hand. I love you, Mama. I love you. Thank you for loving me, for praying for me, and for never giving up on me. Thank you for modeling the importance of staying true to your convictions. Thank you for sending me the book and teaching me how to count gifts. I love the letters you sent me each week with your gratitude list. I started my own, Mom. It's not as long as yours and maybe it won't ever be. It's okay, though. I'm glad to be counting. Thanks for being the best Mom ever. I love you."

Without prompts, the words of love and affirmation continue. Jenny steps around Dan and leans in close to Liz's ear. "Hi Mama, it's me, Jenny. Thank you Mama for letting Mike and me marry last night. You are the one who first told me what a great guy he was. Do you remember that, Mama? Thank you for loving him in the same way you love Mark, Luke, and Ryan. You have welcomed my man into this strange family we have and I am so grateful. I smiled when Mark thanked you for the book. Do you remember the day you gave me a copy? I was working in the office on Dios Basta paperwork. Even though you were so sick from the chemo, you still came to the office every day to thank me for my hard work. One day you handed me the book and said, '*count gifts Jenny, it's the best way to live this thing called life.'* Thank you for the book and for showing me an attitude of gratitude. I love you so much, Mama. I agree with Mark, you are the best mom ever," she gently leans over and kisses Liz's cheek, as Mike reaches around her.

"Liz, it's Mike. I'm here on your left side with Dan and Jenny. Thank you for welcoming me to your family with open arms and hugs every time you see me. And, thank you for entrusting your Jenny to me. Do you remember what you said when I asked for her hand in marriage? You said, '*Micah, you may marry my daughter on one condition. You must always remember that she is a gift to be treasured'* and then you handed me the book. In the front cover, you inscribed, '*to my son, Micah.'* I love you, Liz. Thanks for being Mom to me. Thank you for loving me."

"Aunt Liz, it's Luke. I'm here on your right side with Mom, Mark, Ryan, and Grandma Murphy. Thank you for loving Ryan and me as if we were your own sons. You never differentiated between us and Mark and Jenny. You have blessed me with your love my whole life. I love you more than I have ever said. Thank you for writing to me in Afghanistan and for praying for me. You threw me a great party when I returned. Remember? I'm listening to everyone say 'thank you for the book' knowing that I was going to say those exact words. Do you remember how you signed my book? You signed it '*from your other mother*.' And, Aunt Liz, that is just what you have been to me. Thank you for loving me. I love you."

"Liz, this is Mom Murphy. I'm here right next to Kris,

touching your arm. You've called me Mom Murphy since that day I bowled you over in the dormitory hallway. You've become another daughter to me. I spent much of my life lamenting that I could not have any more children after Kristen was born. You, though, swept into my heart and filled that void. When Don passed away, you and your parents adopted me right in. This Estate became my home because of your generosity. Apparently you have blessed us all with this book. Thank you for the book and for our long conversations over the summer as we tended flowers. You taught me to look for the gifts in the garden. I love you, sweet Liz. Thank you for changing me."

"Aunt Liz, Ryan here. I'm also standing by Mom and Grandma. I can't believe I was born into such an amazing blended family. I've not ever known anything else. Thank you for your part in that. Thank you for loving me as your own son. Luke is right when he said you have never treated us any different than you treated your own children. I can't believe you gave us all the book. When you handed it to me in August, I figured that it was something special. I just didn't know how special it was until I started reading it. Thanks for the letters to college encouraging me to find the gifts in the everyday. I love you, Aunt Liz."

"Lizzie, this is Dan, again. Do you hear us, we are all here with you. I promise you there is not a dry eye in this room. We are all in agreement that you are one amazing lady and we are all blessed because of you. Personally, my list of ways to thank you is long. All those years ago, you stole my heart. It was you who realized that I had fallen for you, but not as one would fall for a lover. You filled the gap my sister left when God called her to heaven at the age of ten. I wept and mourned for eight years and then you swept into my life. It was you who introduced me to this incredible woman I married. You are the one who has held this blended family together. You have taught us much about commitment and generosity. We are all better people for your influence in our lives. I love you my sister, sweet Lizzie."

"Friend, I can think of nothing to add. You are loved and you will be missed, more than words can say. You have stood by me for all of these twenty-eight years. And, now, it is my turn. I will stand by you as you leave. Go with God, dear friend. Be healed and save a place for me. I will be there soon."

In the silence of the room, I realize there is no sound of raspy breathing. I look to Dan and see the tears stream down his face. He nods to me. After a deep breath he says, "Lizzie is with Jesus."

~*~

epilogue

The early morning sunrise paints the sky a thousand colors and more. The golden leaves reflect the sun's rays and light up the cemetery in all the warm colors of fall.

It's been almost a year. A year of more emotions than I ever knew were possible to feel. I miss my friend more now than I did when she slipped from this earth to eternity. I've come to crave these morning walks around this final resting place for so many. My heart knows the way and soon I find that which I seek. The one bench that says...

Solo Dios basta~Solo Dios regala

Liz left us this marble bench as a memorial stone and we have all taken more than one turn to sit here and contemplate these her last words...

God Alone Suffices~God Alone Gifts

Sitting on Liz's memorial bench, I reflect on my list of grace gifts. My list has grown exponentially since my dearest friend took her last earthly breath. A year ago, I wondered how I would live without her. I was completely convinced that I could not breathe without her physical presence. I grossly underestimated the presence of God in my life. I misjudged the measure of God's grace. He has graced me with gifts more numerous than the ones I have counted.

This year without Liz has been a year of rebirth, in a sense, for me. Slowly, I am learning to be as gracious as my friend. God used cancer in her life to teach her to be a grace giver. He's using her death by cancer to teach me. God is too big for me to understand. He sometimes chooses to teach some of us the same lesson in different ways. I am learning to be a grace giver.

I sometimes wonder when Liz realized this secret. At what point, along the way of her journey did she discover that counting gifts of grace leads one to become a grace giver? When did she recognize the change in herself? When did she know it?

I marveled much on the day of Liz's memorial service. She was such a gift to so many people. On that day, my emotions were too thick for me to see Liz's secret. I failed to recognize that she became a gift of grace when she counted gifts of grace.

Kindly and gently, this year, God's Spirit has slowly revealed Liz's secret to me.... life is pain, grace is free, and to whom much grace is given, much grace is required. This very secret is what I am left to share. This secret to living a life of deep and abiding contentment. I have asked God for an opportunity to share this with Liz's children and my own... these four children that we have shared for so many years. Instead of calling all of her gifts around her as I did almost a year ago, I've called them here to gather around her memory. In the gathering, I will share this secret.

I came early this Saturday morning. Jenny and Mike are back from Guatemala, and Ryan is here on his fall break from college. Luke came in last night. Only Mark is missing. He moved to Guatemala to run the mission locally there. I miss him. Yet, I am so proud of him and his journey. Dan and I will go to Mark and Guatemala next week. I am already praying that God will grant an incredible opportunity to share Liz's secret with him there, maybe even as we celebrate the one year anniversary of her birth into heaven.

The subtle crunch of leaves catches my attention. I look up to see the one who holds my heart. He who knows me so well, knew I would come early. Without a word, he sits beside me and tucks my hand into his. An entire conversation takes place without a single word. There is rest in this long love we live.

Together we watch the sun rise and the world awaken. Dan and I wait for the rest to join us. In my free hand, I clutch my Bible. Around this memorial stone on this frosty fall morning, we will gather and remember. This day is one week before the anniversary of her death. And, when we gather and remember, we will worship and praise the One and Only who holds all of life and death in His hands. I will share her secret and we will celebrate her life and the gift that she was to each of us.

Dan releases my hand and stands to see Jenny and Micah round the bend. They carry Hope. Their Hope, the one that has been entrusted to them. We all carry hope these days. Counting gifts has opened our eyes not only to the grace that abounds, but also to the hope that is ours in Jesus Christ. Luke and Ryan come with Mom Murphy right behind the Caldwells. Luke carries fresh calla lilies to lay on Liz's bench.

"From Rob," Luke says, laying the flowers across the bench.

Rob, the one who knows and understands and continues to remember. Instead of remembering Liz's birthday this year, he has chosen to remember the anniversary of the day she slipped into eternity with Jesus. There was a day, not too long ago, that I wished things could have been different for Liz and Rob. Today, I smile at his thoughtfulness and mentally add Rob's grace to my list of gifts.

Gathering around Liz's bench with arms draped over shoulders, we smile and laugh. Tears run freely and it is all good. Twenty-nine years ago, this blended family began with the friendship of two 18-year-old women. Years of the good, the bad, and the ugly woven together to create a bond of love that spans bloodlines and generations. It's in this gathering that we celebrate the gift of Liz and the secret that counting grace gifts leads to grace giving and grace living.

~*~

a note of thanks...

To these and countless others who have come alongside me in this process, thank you seems too small. It is, however, all that I have to give...

~to my Father God... an attitude of gratitude is the best sacrifice of praise I can give. Thank You for Your ongoing work of redemption in my life and for the gift of these words. Without You, I have nothing. To You belongs all glory.

~to my family... Mom, Dad, Gabe, Becky, and Susan, thanks for reading through the messy manuscript to see the story inside. I owe you all some Noa Noa. Eric, Emme and Ellen, thank you for believing in your mom, for praying for me, and for cheering me on. You three inspire me. Chad... there are no words. For all these years, you have gently held my heart and strongly held my hand. Thank you for never letting go!

~to my friends... Ginger and Gwenda, thank you for many, many conversations of pretend people and make-believe places. Ami, Makenna, Rachelle, Emma, and Nikki, thank you for reading and cheering me on. Julie and Kari, thank you for your prayers, friendship and a great photography session! Konda, thank you for the editing and the inspiration. Terry, thanks for sharing your insight and wisdom. My favorite librarians, thanks for spurring me on and believing in me. My favorite bloggers, thanks for being willing to review a manuscript. For all who read rough drafts and commented, thank you!

~*~

Cover art photography rights go to the very talented Kari McGrath Photography. Thanks for sharing your God-given gifts with me! (www.karimcgrath.wordpress.com).

Author photo rights go to the equally talented Marah Grant Photography (www.marahgrant.com).

I am blessed to call you both friend!

All references to 1000 Gifts by Ann Voskamp used with the author's graceful permission. Thank you for the permission, grace, and prayers, Ann!

~*~

about the author

As a mom, wife, and daughter of God, I live a mostly ordinary life in the Midwest. Married eighteen years to the one who holds my heart, I homeschool our youngest daughter having sent our two older children to private and public schools. My days are spent at volleyball practices, football games, homeschool co-op, prayer meetings, softball games, and at my favorite escape—the library. Sometimes I even find time to bake bread, host sledding parties with my kids on snow days, and swim at our local community pool. I have played in a F.R.O.G. and ridden in a Mighty Truck. I have also prayed many friends through the horrific battle of breast cancer. My life is richer for the gift of these friends.

In some form or another, I have imagined, shared, told, and written stories for as long as I can remember. Being called to share my stories has been a journey out of the ordinary for me. This is my first published novel. I am immensely grateful for this gift to craft words into stories. It is simply a gift. All credit goes to my

Creator and Savior, Jesus Christ. It is to Him that I continue to count grace gifts every day.

More of my thoughts, stories, and a collection of my free Bible studies for children, teens, and families can be found on my blog www.heidikreider.com.

I would love to hear from you! Please email me (kreidermom@yahoo.com) if you have any comments or suggestions or if you want to share how this book has changed you.

Thank you, Friend!

~*~

18293729R00181

Made in the USA
Middletown, DE
02 March 2015